'So how do you *pr* intended—to mak Hannah informed asperity, 'that I'm actually thinking of going along with this idea.'

'Of course not,' Luca murmured.

Hannah watched, mesmerised, as he tugged off his tie and then began to unbutton his shirt. 'What are you doing?' she squeaked.

'Changing. We're due for cocktails in an hour.'

'Can't you use the bathroom—?' She nodded towards the door that led to what looked like a sumptuous en suite.

'Why should I?' Luca's smile was wicked. 'We're engaged to be married, after all.'

Hannah took a deep breath. 'So, you still haven't told me how this is going to work.'

'We're going to act like we're engaged. Simple.'

'Simple?' She opened her eyes to glare at Luca. He stood across the room, buckling the belt on a pair of grey trousers. His chest was still gloriously bare. 'It's not *simple*, Luca. We're not engaged. We barely know each other. If someone asks either one of us anything about our relationship or how we met we'll have no idea what to say.'

'It's best to keep as close to the truth as possible,' Luca advised as he reached for a light blue shirt and shrugged into it. 'You're still my PA.'

'And we just happen to be engaged? Convenient.'

He shot her a quick, hard smile. 'It is, isn't it?'

After spending three years as a die-hard New Yorker, **Kate Hewitt** now lives in a small village in the English Lake District with her husband, their five children and a golden retriever. In addition to writing intensely emotional stories, she loves reading, baking and playing chess with her son—she has yet to win against him, but she continues to try. Learn more about Kate at kate-hewitt.com.

Books by Kate Hewitt

Mills & Boon Modern Romance

Inherited by Ferranti
Kholodov's Last Mistress
The Undoing of de Luca

One Night With Consequences

Larenzo's Christmas Baby

The Marakaios Brides

The Marakaios Marriage
The Marakaios Baby

The Chatsfield

Virgin's Sweet Rebellion

Rivals to the Crown of Kadar

Captured by the Sheikh
Commanded by the Sheikh

The Diomedi Heirs

The Prince She Never Knew
A Queen for the Taking?

The Bryants: Powerful & Proud

Beneath the Veil of Paradise
In the Heat of the Spotlight
His Brand of Passion

Visit the Author Profile page
at millsandboon.co.uk for more titles.

MORETTI'S MARRIAGE COMMAND

BY

KATE HEWITT

All rights reserved including the right of reproduction in whole or in part in any form. This edition is published by arrangement with Harlequin Books S.A.

This is a work of fiction. Names, characters, places, locations and incidents are purely fictional and bear no relationship to any real life individuals, living or dead, or to any actual places, business establishments, locations, events or incidents. Any resemblance is entirely coincidental.

This book is sold subject to the condition that it shall not, by way of trade or otherwise, be lent, resold, hired out or otherwise circulated without the prior consent of the publisher in any form of binding or cover other than that in which it is published and without a similar condition including this condition being imposed on the subsequent purchaser.

® and TM are trademarks owned and used by the trademark owner and/or its licensee. Trademarks marked with ® are registered with the United Kingdom Patent Office and/or the Office for Harmonisation in the Internal Market and in other countries.

First Published in Great Britain 2016
By Mills & Boon, an imprint of HarperCollins*Publishers*
1 London Bridge Street, London, SE1 9GF

© 2016 Kate Hewitt

ISBN: 978-0-263-06483-4

Our policy is to use papers that are natural, renewable and recyclable produ[illegible] own in sust[illegible]able forests. The logging and manufacturing processes conform to the legal environmental regulations of the country of origin.

Printed and bound in Great Britain
by CPI Antony Rowe, Chippenham, Wiltshire

LIBRARIES NI

C900054346

MAG 14.10.16

AF £14.50

BAS

MORETTI'S MARRIAGE COMMAND

To all my readers.
Thank you for your encouragement and support.
It’s always a privilege to write stories for you.

CHAPTER ONE

LUCA MORETTI NEEDED a wife. Not a real one—heaven forbid he'd ever need *that.* No, he needed a temporary wife-to-be who was efficient, biddable, and discreet. A wife for the weekend.

'Mr Moretti?' His PA, Hannah Stewart, knocked once on the door before opening it and stepping inside his penthouse office overlooking a rain-washed Lombard Street in London's City. 'I have the letters for you to sign.'

Luca watched his PA walk towards him holding the sheaf of letters, her light brown hair neatly pulled back, her face set in calm lines. She wore a black pencil skirt, low heels, and a simple blouse of white silk. He'd never really bothered to notice his PA before, except at how quickly she could type and how discreet she could be when it came to unfortunate personal calls that occasionally came through to his office. Now he eyed her plain brown hair, and lightly freckled face that was pretty without being in any way remarkable. As for her figure…?

Luca let his gaze wander down his PA's slender form. No breathtaking or bodacious curves, but it was passable.

Could he...?

She placed the letters in front of him and took a step back, but not before he caught a waft of her understated floral perfume. He reached for his fountain pen and began to scrawl his signature on each letter.

'Will that be all, Mr Moretti?' she asked when he'd finished the last one.

'Yes.' He handed her the letters and Hannah turned towards the door, her skirt whispering against her legs as she walked. Luca watched her, eyes narrowed, certainty settling in his gut. 'Wait.'

Obedient as ever, Hannah pivoted back to face him, her pale eyebrows raised expectantly. She'd been a good PA these last three years, working hard and not making a fuss about it. He sensed ambition and willpower beneath her 'aiming to please' persona, and the weekend would require both qualities, as long as she agreed to the deception. Which he would make sure she did.

'Mr Moretti?'

Luca lounged back in his chair as he drummed his fingers on his desk. He didn't like lying. He'd been honest his whole life, proud of who he was even though so many had knocked him back, tried to keep him down. But this weekend was different. This weekend was everything to him, and Hannah Stewart was no more than a cog in his plans. A very important cog.

'I have an important meeting this weekend.'

'Yes, on Santa Nicola,' Hannah replied. 'Your ticket is in your passport wallet, and the limo is set to pick you up tomorrow morning at nine, from your flat. The flight leaves from Heathrow at noon.'

'Right.' He hadn't known any of those details, but he'd expected Hannah to inform him. She really was quite marvellously efficient. 'It turns out I'm going to need some assistance,' he said.

Hannah's eyebrows went a fraction higher, but her face remained calm. 'Administrative assistance, you mean?'

Luca hesitated. He didn't have time to explain his intentions now, and he suspected that his PA would balk at what he was about to ask. 'Yes, that's right.' He could tell Hannah was surprised although she hid it well.

'What exactly do you require?'

A wife. A temporary, compliant woman. 'I require you to accompany me to Santa Nicola for the weekend.' Luca hadn't asked Hannah to accompany him on any business trips before; he preferred to travel and work alone, having been a solitary person from childhood. When you were alone you didn't have to be on your guard, waiting for someone to trip you up. There were no expectations save the ones you put on yourself.

Luca knew that Hannah's contract stipulated 'extra hours or engagements as required', and in the past she'd been willing to work long evenings, the occasional Saturday. He smiled, his eyebrows raised expectantly. 'I trust that won't be a problem?' He would inform her later just what extra duties would be required.

Hannah hesitated, but only briefly, and then gave one graceful nod of her head. 'Not at all, Mr Moretti.'

Hannah's mind raced as she tried to figure out how to handle this unexpected request from her boss. In her three years of working for Luca Moretti, she'd never gone on a business trip with him. There had been the odd, or not so odd, late night; the occasional all-nighter where she supplied him with black coffee and popped caffeine pills to keep sharp as she took notes. But she'd never *travelled* with him. Never gone somewhere as exotic as a Mediterranean island for the weekend. The possibility gave her a surprising frisson of excitement; she'd thought she'd put her would-be travelling days behind her long ago.

'Shall I book an extra ticket?' she asked, trying to sound as efficient and capable as she always was.

'Yes.'

She nodded, her mind still spinning. She needed to call her mother as soon as possible, make arrangements… 'I'll book an economy ticket—'

'Why on earth would you do that?' Luca demanded. He sounded irritated, and Hannah blinked in surprise.

'I hardly think, as your PA, I'd need to travel first class, and the expense—'

'Forget the expense.' He cut her off, waving a hand in dismissal. 'I'll need you seated with me. I'll work on the flight.'

'Very well.' She held the letters to her chest, wondering what else she'd need to do to prepare for such a trip. And wondering why Luca Moretti needed her on this trip when he hadn't needed her on any other. She studied him covertly, lounging as he was in his office chair, his midnight-dark hair rumpled, his thick, straight brows drawn into frowning lines, one hand still drumming the top of his ebony desk.

He was an incredibly handsome man, a compelling, charismatic, driven man; one business magazine had called him 'an elegant steamroller'. Hannah thought the nickname apt; Luca Moretti could turn on the charm, but it was only to get what he wanted. She'd observed him from the sidelines for three years and learned how to be the most efficient PA possible, and invisible when necessary. She liked her job; she liked Luca's force of personality, his boundless energy for his work. She'd always admired his determined work ethic, his drive for success. She might only be a PA, but she shared that drive, if not quite to the same degree.

'Very well,' she said now. 'I'll make the arrangements.' Luca nodded her dismissal and Hannah left his office, expelling her breath in a rush as she sat down at her desk. She and Luca were the only occupants of the top floor of his office building, and she appreciated the quiet to organise her thoughts.

First things first. She called the airline and booked an additional first-class ticket for herself, wincing at the expense even though Luca Moretti could well afford it. As CEO of his own real-estate development empire, he could have afforded his own jet.

That done, she quickly emailed her mother. She would have called, but Luca forbade personal calls from the office, and Hannah had always obeyed the rules. This job meant too much to her to flaunt them. She'd just hit Send when Luca emerged from his office, shrugging on his suit jacket and checking his watch.

'Mr Moretti?'

'You'll need suitable clothes for this weekend.'

Hannah blinked. 'Of course.'

'I don't mean that.' Luca gestured to her clothes, and Hannah was unable to keep from looking down at her professional yet understated outfit. She took pride in how she dressed, and she made sure to buy as high quality clothes as she could afford.

'I'm sorry…?'

'This weekend is as much a social occasion as a business one,' he explained tersely. 'You'll need appropriate clothing—evening gowns and the like.'

Evening gowns? She certainly didn't have any of those in her wardrobe, and couldn't imagine the need for them. 'As your PA—'

'As my PA you need to be dressed appropriately. This isn't going to be a board meeting.'

'What is it, exactly? Because I'm not sure—'

'Think of it more as a weekend house party with a little business thrown in.'

Which made it even more mystifying as to why he needed her along.

'I'm afraid I don't own any evening gowns—' Hannah began, and Luca shrugged her words aside.

'That's easy enough to take care of.' He slid his smartphone out of his pocket and thumbed a few buttons before speaking rapidly in Italian. Although she heard the occasional familiar word, Hannah had no idea what he'd said or who he'd called.

A few minutes later he disconnected the call and nodded towards Hannah. 'Sorted. You'll accompany me to Diavola after work.'

'Diavola…?'

'You know the boutique?'

She'd heard of it. It was an incredibly high-end fashion boutique in Mayfair. She might have walked past the elegant sashed windows once, seen a single dress hanging there in an elegant fall of shimmery silk, no price tag visible.

She swallowed hard, striving to seem calm, as if this whole, unexpected venture hadn't completely thrown her. 'That might be a bit out of my price range—'

'I will pay, of course.' His brows snapped together as he frowned at her. 'It's all part of the business expense. I'd hardly expect you to buy a gown you'll only be wearing because of your work.'

'Very well.' She tried not to squirm under his fierce gaze. She felt as if he was examining her and she was not meeting his expectations, which was disconcerting, as she always had before. She took pride in how well she performed her job. Luca Moretti had never had any cause to criticise her. 'Thank you.'

'We'll leave in an hour,' Luca said, and strode back into his office.

Hannah spent a frantic hour finishing up her work and making arrangements for the trip, ensuring that each part of the journey could accommodate an extra passenger. She knew Luca was staying with his client, hotelier Andrew Tyson, and she hesitated to contact the man directly to make sure there was an extra bedroom. It seemed a bit cheeky, asking for a room for herself in the tycoon's luxurious villa, but what else could she do?

She was just composing an email to Andrew Tyson's PA when Luca came out of his office, shrugging into his suit jacket, his face settling into a frown as he caught sight of her.

'Aren't you ready?'

'I'm sorry, I'm just emailing Mr Tyson's PA—'

His frown deepened. 'What for?'

'To arrange for an extra bedroom—'

'That won't be necessary,' Luca said swiftly, and then leaned over and closed her laptop with a snap.

Hannah stared at him, too surprised to mask the emotion. 'But if I don't email—'

'It's taken care of.'

'It is?'

'Don't question me, Hannah. And in future please leave all communications with Mr Tyson to me.'

Stung, she recoiled a bit at his tone. 'I've always—'

'This negotiation is delicate. I'll explain the particulars later. Now let's go. I have a lot of things to do tonight besides buy you some clothes.'

Her cheeks burned at his dismissive tone. Her boss was often restless and impatient, but he wasn't *rude.* Was it her fault that her wardrobe wasn't that of a socialite? Wordlessly she rose from her desk and took her laptop, about to slide it into her messenger bag.

'Leave that.'

'My laptop?' She stared at him, flummoxed. 'But I'll need it if we're to work on the plane—'

'It won't be necessary.'

A finger of unease crept along her spine. Something felt very off about this weekend, and yet she could not imagine what it was. 'Mr Moretti, I don't understand...'

'What is there to understand? You're accompanying me on a weekend that is as much a social occasion as it is a business one. I'm asking you to use some sensitivity and discretion, as the situation is delicate. Is that beyond your capabilities, Miss Stewart?'

Her face burned at being given such a dressing-down. 'No, of course not.'

'Good.' He nodded towards the lift doors. 'Now let's go.'

Stiff with affront, Hannah took her coat and followed Luca to the lift. She waited, staring straight ahead, trying to master her irritation, until the doors pinged open and Luca gestured for her to go in first. She did so, and as he followed her she was conscious in an entirely new way of how he filled the space of the lift. Surely they'd ridden in the lift together before, many times. Yet now, as Luca stabbed the button for the ground floor, she felt how big he was. How male. His shoulders strained the seams of his suit jacket, and his rangy, restless energy made the very air seem as if it were charged. She snuck a glance at his profile, the square jaw shadowed with stubble, the straight nose and angular cheekbones. Long, surprisingly lush lashes, and hard, dark eyes.

Hannah knew women flocked to Luca Moretti. They were attracted to his air of restless remoteness as much as his blatant sexuality and effortless charisma. Perhaps they fooled themselves into thinking they could tame or trap him; no one ever could. Hannah had kept more than one tearful beauty from her boss's door. He never thanked her for that little service; he acted as if the women who practically threw themselves at him didn't exist, at least not outside the bedroom. Or so Hannah assumed—she had no idea how Luca Moretti acted in the bedroom.

Just the thought sent a blush heating her cheeks now, even though she was still annoyed with his uncharacteristically terse attitude. High-handed she could take, when it was tempered with wry charm and grace. But Luca Moretti merely barking out orders was hard to stomach.

Thankfully the doors opened and they left the confined space of the lift, Luca ushering her out into the impressive marble foyer of Moretti Enterprises. A receptionist bid them good day and then they were out in the rain-washed streets, the damp air cooling her face, the twilight hiding her blush.

A limo pulled to the kerb the moment they stepped out, and Luca's driver jumped out to open the door.

'After you,' Luca said, and Hannah slid inside the luxurious interior. Luca followed, his thigh nudging hers before he shifted closer to the window.

Hannah couldn't resist stroking the buttery soft leather of the seat. 'I've never been in a limo before,' she admitted, and Luca cocked an eyebrow at her.

'Never?'

'No.' Why would she? He might travel in this sort of style all over the world, but she stayed firmly on the top floor of Moretti Enterprises. Of course, she'd seen plenty of luxury from a distance. She'd ordered champagne to celebrate his business deals, heard the pop of the cork in the meeting room down from his office. She'd booked dozens of first-class tickets and five-star hotel rooms, had instructed concierges around the world on Luca Moretti's preferences: no lilies in any flower arrangements in his suite and sheets with a five hundred thread count. She'd just never experienced any of that expense or luxury herself. 'I haven't stayed in a five-star hotel or flown first class either,' she informed him a bit tartly. Not everyone was as privileged as he was. 'I haven't even tasted champagne.'

'Well, you can enjoy some of that this weekend,' Luca said, and turned to stare out of the window, the lights from the traffic casting his face in a yellow wash. 'I'm sorry,' he said abruptly. 'I know I must seem…tense.'

Hannah eyed him warily. 'Ye—es…'

He turned to her with a small, rueful smile. 'I think that was an inward "you've been an absolute rotter".' His expression softened, his gaze sweeping over her, lashes lowering in a way that made Hannah feel the need to shift in her seat. 'I am sorry.'

'Why are you so tense?'

'As I said before, this weekend is delicate.' He turned back to the window, one long-fingered hand rubbing his jaw. 'Very delicate.'

Hannah knew better than to press. She had no idea why this business deal was so delicate; as far as she could tell, the chain of family resort hotels Luca was planning to take over was a relatively small addition to his real-estate portfolio.

The limo pulled up to Diavola, the windows lit although it was nearly seven o'clock at night. Hannah suppressed a shiver of apprehension. How was this supposed to *work*? Would she choose the dress, or would her boss? She'd done many things for Luca Moretti, but she hadn't bought herself an evening gown for him. She didn't relish the idea of parading clothes in front of him, but maybe he'd just let her choose a gown and get on with it.

Of course he would. He was already impatient, wanting to get onto the next thing; Luca Moretti wasn't going to entertain himself watching his PA try on different dresses. Comforted by this thought, Hannah slid out of the limo.

Luca followed her quickly, placing one hand on her elbow. The touch shocked her; Luca *never* touched her. Not so much as a hug or a pat on the back in three years of working for him. Hannah had always got the sense that he was a solitary man, despite the parade of women through his life, and she hadn't minded because she appreciated the focus on work. She didn't have room in her life for much else.

Now Luca kept his hand on her elbow as he guided her into the boutique, and then slid it to the small of her back as a shop assistant came forward. Hannah felt as if he were branding her back, his palm warm through the thin material of her skirt, his fingers splayed so she could feel the light yet firm pressure of each one. His pinkie finger reached the curve of her bottom, and her whole body stiffened in response as a treacherous flash of heat jolted through her.

'I would like a complete wardrobe for the weekend for my companion,' he said to the woman, who batted over-mascaraed lashes at him. 'Evening gowns, day wear, a swimming costume, nightgown, underthings.' He glanced at the gold and silver watch on one wrist. 'In under an hour.'

'Very good, Mr Moretti.'

Underthings? Hannah felt she had to object. 'Mr Moretti, I don't need all those things,' she protested in a low voice. She certainly didn't need her boss to buy her a bra. She felt the pressure on the small of her back increase, so she could feel the joints of each of his fingers.

'Humour me. And why don't you call me Luca?' Her jaw nearly dropped at this suggestion. He'd never invited such intimacy before. 'You've been working for me for what, three years?' he murmured so only she could hear, his head close enough to hers that she breathed in the cedarwood-scented aftershave he wore. When she turned her head she could see the hint of stubble on his jaw. 'Perhaps we should progress to first names… Hannah.'

For some reason her name on his lips made her want to shiver. She stepped away from his hand, her body bizarrely missing the warmth and pressure of it as soon as it had gone.

'Very well.' Yet she couldn't quite make herself call

him Luca. It seemed so odd, so intimate, after three years of starchy formality and respectable distance. Why was Luca shaking everything up now?

The sales assistant was collecting various garments from around the boutique, and another had come forward to usher them both to a U-shaped divan in cream velvet. A third was bringing flutes of champagne and caviar-topped crackers.

Luca sat down, clearly accustomed to all this luxury, and the sales assistant beckoned to Hannah.

'If the *signorina* will come this way…?'

Numbly Hannah followed the woman into a dressing room that was larger than the entire upstairs of her house.

'First this?' the woman suggested, holding up an evening gown in pale blue chiffon and satin. It was the most exquisite thing Hannah had ever seen.

'Okay,' she said, and, feeling as if she were in a surreal dream, she started to unbutton her blouse.

CHAPTER TWO

LUCA WAITED FOR Hannah to emerge from the dressing room as he sipped champagne and tried to relax. He was way too wound up about this whole endeavour, and his too-clever PA had noticed. He didn't want her guessing his game before they'd arrived on Santa Nicola. He couldn't risk the possibility of her refusal. Although Hannah Stewart had proved to be biddable enough, he suspected she had more backbone than he'd initially realised. And he didn't want her to use it against him.

Moodily Luca took a sip of champagne and stared out at the rainy streets of Mayfair. In less than twenty-four hours he'd be on Santa Nicola, facing Andrew Tyson. Would the man recognise him? It had been such a long time. Would there be so much as a flicker of awareness in those cold eyes? If there was it would completely ruin Luca's plan, and yet he couldn't keep from hoping that he would garner some reaction. Something to justify the emotion that had burned in his chest for far too long.

'Well?' he called to Hannah. She'd been in the dressing room for nearly ten minutes. 'Have you tried something on?'

'Yes, but this one's a bit…' She trailed off, and Luca snapped his gaze to the heavy velvet curtain drawn across the dressing room's doorway.

'Come out and let me see it.'

'It's fine.' She sounded a little panicked but also quite firm. 'I'll try something else on—'

'Hannah.' Luca tried to curb his impatience. 'I would like to see the dress, please.' What woman didn't enjoy showing off haute couture for a man? And he needed to make sure Hannah looked the part.

'I'm already changing,' she called, and in one fluid movement Luca rose from the divan and crossed to the dressing room, pulling aside the heavy curtain.

He didn't know who gasped—Hannah, in shock that he'd intruded, or himself, for the sudden dart of lust that had arrowed through his body at the sight of his PA.

She stood with her back to him, the dress pooling about her waist in gauzy blue folds as she held the front up to her chest, her face in profile, every inch the outraged maiden.

'Mr Moretti—' she muttered and he watched a blush crawl up her back and neck to her face.

'Luca,' he reminded her, and sent an iron glare of warning to the assistant, who was waiting discreetly in the corner. He did not want anyone gossiping about the oddity of the occasion.

'Luca,' Hannah acquiesced, but she sounded annoyed. Luca felt a surprising flicker of amusement. His little sparrow of a secretary sometimes pretended she was a hawk. 'Please leave. I am *changing*.'

'I wanted to see the gown. I'm paying for it, after all.' He folded his arms, feeling no more than a flash of remorse for pulling that particular trump card. Hannah, however, did not look particularly impressed. 'How much is this gown?' he asked the sales assistant.

The woman hesitated, but only for a millisecond. 'Nine thousand pounds, Signor Moretti.'

'Nine thousand—' Hannah whirled around, the dress nearly slipping from her hands. Luca caught a glimpse of pale, lightly freckled fresh, the hint of a small, perfectly round breast. Then she hauled the gown up to her chin, her face now bright red with mortification.

'Careful,' he advised. 'That material looks delicate.'

'As delicate as this weekend?' she retorted, and he smiled.

'I never knew you had a temper.'

'I never knew you could spend nine thousand pounds on a *dress*.'

He raised his eyebrows, genuinely surprised. 'Most women of my acquaintance enjoy spending my money.'

'Your acquaintance is quite limited, then,' Hannah snapped. 'Plenty of women aren't interested only in shopping and money.'

'Point taken.'

'Anyway,' Hannah muttered, 'it's wrong.' She turned around so her back was once more to him.

'Wrong? But how can you object if it's my money?'

'Do you know what could be done with nine thousand pounds?' she demanded, her back straight and quivering with tension.

'Oh, no, tell me you're not one of those bleeding hearts,' Luca drawled. 'I expected more of you, Hannah.'

'I'm not,' she said stiffly. 'I've never objected to you spending money on yourself. But when it's for me—'

'It's still my choice.' He cut her off. 'Now zip up that dress and let me see it on you.'

Taking her cue, the sales assistant stepped forward and zipped up the back, although in truth there wasn't much to zip up. The dress was almost entirely backless, with a halter top and a gauzy chiffon overlay that lent some respectability to the plunging neckline, as Luca saw when Hannah reluctantly turned around.

He schooled his face into an expression of businesslike interest, as if he were assessing the gown simply as an appropriate garment for the occasion rather than for the effect it had on his libido. Why on earth he was reacting to his PA's unexceptional body this way he had no idea. He supposed that was what you paid for with Diavola. The dresses worked.

'Very good,' he told the assistant. 'We'll take it. Now we need something casual to wear for the day, and a semi-formal dress for the first night.'

'I have some of these things at home,' Hannah protested.

Luca held up a hand. 'Please cease this pointless arguing, Hannah. This is a business expense, I told you.'

She went silent, tight-lipped, her brown eyes flashing suppressed fury. Unable to resist baiting her just a little bit, or maybe just wanting to touch her, Luca reached over and pulled the tie of the halter top of her dress.

'There,' he said as she caught the folds of the dress, her eyes wide with shock. 'Now hurry up. I want to be out of here in forty-five minutes.'

Hannah's hands trembled as she stripped off the evening gown and flung it at the assistant, too unsettled and overwhelmed to care how she treated the delicate material.

What was going on? Why was Luca treating her this way? And why had she reacted to the sight of him in the dressing room, her body tightening, heat flaring deep inside when she'd turned around and seen his gaze dip to her unimpressive cleavage?

Perhaps, she thought resentfully, she'd simply never seen this side of her boss before. Outside the office, Luca Moretti might well be the kind of man who flirted and teased and stormed into women's dressing rooms and undid their gowns…

She suppressed a shiver at the memory of his fingers skimming her back as he'd tugged on the tie. Stupid, to react to the man that way. At this moment she wasn't even sure she liked him. And yet it had been a long, long time since she'd been touched like that.

Not, of course, that Luca had had any intention other than discomfiting her when he'd undone her dress. Hannah was savvy enough to realise that.

And as for the cost... Maybe it was irrational to protest when a millionaire spent what was essentially pocket change, but it was a lot of money to her. With nine thousand pounds she could have redone her kitchen or afforded a better life insurance policy...

'*Signorina?* Would you like to try on the next ensemble?'

Letting out a long, low breath, Hannah nodded. 'Yes, please.' This whole evening had entered into the realm of the utterly surreal, including her own reactions. When had she ever dared to talk back to her boss? Yet he didn't feel like her boss when she was in a dressing room, her back bare, her breasts practically on display. And yet at the same time he felt more like her boss than ever, demanding and autocratic, expecting instant compliance. It was all so incredibly bizarre.

The assistant handed her a shift dress in pale pink linen that fitted perfectly. Would Luca want to see this dress as well? And what about her swimming costume, or the lacy, frothy underthings she could see waiting on a chair? A blaze of heat went through her at the thought, leaving her more disconcerted than ever.

'It's fine,' she told the assistant, and then took it off as fast as she could. Maybe if she worked quickly enough Luca wouldn't bother striding into her dressing room, acting as if he owned the world, acting as if he owned *her.*

Forty-two minutes later all the clothes Hannah had tried on, including the most modest bikini she'd been able to find and two sets of lingerie in beige silk and cream lace, were wrapped in tissue paper and put in expensive-looking bags with satin ribbons for handles. She hadn't even seen Luca hand over a credit card, and she dreaded to think what the bill was. Why on earth was he spending a fortune on her clothes, and for such a negligible business deal? She didn't like feeling beholden to him in such a way. She worked hard and earned everything she got, and she preferred it like that.

'I think you've spent more on me tonight than you'll make taking over these resorts,' she remarked as they stepped out into the street. The rain had cleared and a pale sickle moon rose above the elegant town houses of Mayfair. 'Andrew Tyson only owns about half a dozen resorts, doesn't he?'

'The land alone makes it worth it,' Luca replied, buttoning his jacket. Seconds later the limo appeared at the kerb, and the sales assistant loaded the bags into the boot.

'I should get home,' Hannah said. She felt relieved at the thought of being away from Luca's unsettling presence, and yet reluctant to end the bizarre magic of the evening. But it was a forty-five-minute Tube ride to her small terraced house on the end of the Northern Line, and she'd be late enough as it was.

'I'll drive you,' Luca answered. 'Get in.'

'I live rather far away…'

'I know where you live.'

His calm assertion discomfited her. Of course her boss knew where she lived; it was on her employment record. And yet the thought of Luca invading her home, seeing even just a glimpse her private life, made her resist.

'I don't…'

'Hannah, get in. It's nearly eight and we're leaving at nine tomorrow morning. Why spend nearly an hour on the Tube when you don't have to?'

He had a point. As it was she'd be getting back later than she liked. 'All right, thank you.' She climbed into the limo, sitting well away from Luca. She could still remember the feel of his fingers on her back. *Stupid, stupid, stupid.* He'd probably been amused at how embarrassed she'd been. He probably undressed women in his sleep. The only reason she'd responded to him like that was because he was attractive and she hadn't been touched by a man in over five years. Her mother had told her it was more than time to jump back in the dating pool, but Hannah hadn't had time even to think about dipping a toe in.

The limo pulled into the street and Hannah sat back, suddenly overwhelmed with fatigue. The last few hours had taken an emotional toll.

'Here.' Luca pressed a glass into her hands, and her fingers closed around the fragile stem automatically. She looked in surprise at the flute of champagne. The driver must have had it ready. 'You didn't have any in the boutique,' Luca explained, 'and you said you had never tasted it before.'

'Oh.' She was touched by his thoughtfulness, and yet she felt weirdly exposed too. When had her boss ever considered what she wanted in such a way? 'Thank you.'

'Drink,' Luca said, and Hannah took a cautious sip, wrinkling her nose as the bubbles fizzed their way upward. Luca smiled at her faintly, no doubt amused by her inexperience.

'It's a bit more tickly than I thought,' she said. She felt incredibly gauche. Luca had most likely first imbibed Dom Perignon from a baby's bottle. He kept a bottle in his limo, after all. And here she was, saying how the bubbles tickled her nose.

She handed back the champagne with an awkward smile, and Luca took it, one dark eyebrow arched. 'Is it not to your liking?'

'It's just…I haven't eaten anything. And you know, alcohol on an empty stomach, never a good idea…' She was babbling, out of her element in so many ways. She, the calm, capable, unflappable PA, had been reduced to stammering and blushing by her boss, who was acting more like a man than an employer. She couldn't understand him or herself, and it was incredibly annoying.

'I'm sorry,' Luca murmured. 'I should have thought.' He pressed the intercom button and issued some directions in Italian. Hannah eyed him askance.

'What are you doing…?'

'I asked him to stop so we can eat. You don't have plans?'

Surprised alarm had her lurching upright. 'No, but really, it's not necessary—'

'Hannah, you're hungry. When you work late at the office, I provide dinner. Consider this the same thing.'

Except this didn't *feel* like the same thing. And when the limo stopped in front of an elegant bistro with red velvet curtains in the windows and curling gold script on the door, Hannah knew their meal would be a far cry from the sandwiches and coffee Luca usually had her order in when they were both working late.

She swallowed audibly, and then forced back the feelings of uncertainty and inadequacy. She'd been working as PA to one of the most powerful men in real estate for three years. She could handle dinner at a restaurant.

Straightening her spine, she got out of the car. Luca opened the door to the restaurant for her and then followed her in. The muted, understated elegance of the place fell over her like a soothing blanket.

'A table for two, Monsieur Moretti?' The French waiter asked, menus already in hand. Was her boss known *everywhere*?

Luca nodded and within seconds they were escorted to a private table in the corner, tucked away from the few other diners in the restaurant.

Hannah scanned the menu; it provided a temporary escape from Luca's penetrating gaze. *Foie gras. Roasted quail. Braised fillet of brill.* Okay, she could do this.

'Do you see something you like?' Luca asked.

'Yes.' She closed the menu and gave him a perfunctory smile. 'Thank you.'

The waiter came with the wine list, and Luca barely glanced at it before ordering a bottle. He turned to Hannah the moment the man had gone, his gaze resting on her. Again she had the sense of coming up short, of not being quite what he wanted, and she didn't understand it.

'It occurs to me that I know very little about you.'

'I didn't realise you wanted to,' Hannah answered. Luca had never asked her a single personal question in her three years of employment.

'Information is always valuable,' he answered with a negligent shrug. 'Where did you grow up?'

'A village outside Birmingham.' She eyed him warily. Where was this coming from? And why?

'Brothers? Sisters?'

'No.' Deciding this could go both ways, Hannah raised her eyebrows. 'What about you?'

Luca looked slightly taken aback, his eyes flaring, mouth compressing. In the dim lighting of the restaurant he looked darker and more alluring than usual, the candlelight from the table throwing his face into stark contrast from the snowy whiteness of his shirt, his whole being exuding restless power, barely leashed energy. 'What about me?'

'Do you have brothers or sisters?'

His mouth flattened into a hard line and he looked away briefly. 'No.'

So apparently he didn't like answering personal questions, just asking them. Hannah couldn't say she was surprised. The waiter came to take their order, and she chose a simple salad and the roasted quail, which she hoped would taste like chicken. Luca ordered steak and then the sommelier was proffering an expensive-looking bottle. Hannah watched as Luca expertly swilled a mouthful and then nodded in acceptance. The sommelier poured them both full glasses.

'I really shouldn't…' Hannah began. She didn't drink alcohol very often and she wanted to be fresh for tomorrow. And she didn't relish getting a bit of a buzz in Luca's presence. The last thing she needed was to feel even sillier in front of her boss.

'It won't be on an empty stomach,' Luca replied. 'And I think you need to relax.'

'Do you?' Hannah returned tartly. 'I must confess, this is all a bit out of the ordinary, Mr—'

'Luca.'

'Why?' she burst out. 'Why now?'

His dark gaze rested on her for a moment, and she had the sense he was weighing his words, choosing them with care. 'Why not?' he finally replied, and reached for his wine glass. Hannah deflated, frustrated but also a tiny bit relieved by his non-answer. She didn't know if she could handle some sort of weird revelation.

Fortunately Luca stopped with the personal questions after that, and they ate their meal mainly in silence, which was far more comfortable than being the subject of her boss's scrutiny, but even so she felt on edge, brittle and restless.

Which was too bad, she realised as Luca was paying the bill, because, really, she'd just had the most amazing evening—being bought a designer wardrobe and then treated to a fantastic meal by an undeniably sexy and charismatic man. Too bad it didn't feel like that. It felt…weird. Like something she could enjoy if she let herself, but she didn't think she should. Luca Moretti might have dozens of women at his beck and call, at his feet, but Hannah didn't intend to be one of them. Not if she wanted to keep her job, not to mention her sanity.

They drove in silence to her little house; by the time they'd arrived it was nearly ten o'clock. Her mother, Hannah thought with a flash of guilt, would be both tired and worried.

'I'll see you here tomorrow at nine,' Luca said, and Hannah turned to him in surprise.

'I thought I would be making my own way to the airport.'

'By Tube? And what if you're later? It's better this way. Here, let me get your bags.'

Hannah groped for her keys while Luca took the bags from the boutique to her doorstep. 'Thank you,' she muttered. 'You can go—'

But he was waiting for her to open her front door. She fumbled with the key, breathing a sigh of relief when the door finally swung open.

'Hannah?' her mother called. 'I've been wondering where you were—'

'I'm fine—' Hannah turned to Luca, practically grabbing the bags from him. 'Thank you very much. I'll see you tomorrow at nine.'

He was frowning, his gaze moving from her to the narrow hallway behind her, her mother coming around the corner. Clearly he was wondering about her living situation.

'Goodnight,' Hannah said, and closed the door.

Her mother, Diane, stopped short, her eyes widening as she saw all the expensive-looking bags by Hannah's feet. 'What on earth…?'

'It's a long story,' Hannah said. 'Sorry I'm so late. Did Jamie…?'

'Went to bed without a whimper, bless him,' Diane said. Her gaze moved to the bags. 'Goodness, that's a lot of shopping.'

'Yes, it is,' Hannah agreed rather grimly. 'Let me go see Jamie and then I'll tell you all about it.' Or at least some of it. She'd probably omit a few details, like Luca undoing her dress. The memory alone was enough to make a shiver go through her. Again.

'I'll make you a cup of tea,' Diane said. Hannah was already heading up the narrow stairway and then down the darkened hall to the small second bedroom. She tiptoed inside, her heart lifting at the familiar and beloved sight: her son. He slept on his back, arms and legs flung out like a starfish, his breathing deep and even.

Gently Hannah reached down and brushed the sandy hair from his forehead, her fingers skimming his plump, baby-soft cheek. He was five years old and the light of her life. And she wouldn't see him for a whole weekend.

Guilt niggled at her at the thought. Hannah knew her job was demanding and she wasn't able to spend as much time with Jamie as she would like. She also knew, all too well, the importance of financial independence and freedom. Working for Luca Moretti had given her both. She would never regret making that choice.

With a soft sigh Hannah leaned down and kissed her son's forehead, and then quietly left the room. She needed to get ready for her weekend with her boss.

CHAPTER THREE

LUCA DRUMMED HIS fingers against his thigh as the limo pulled up in front of Hannah's house. He'd been there less than twelve hours ago, dropping her off after their shopping and meal. He'd been strangely disquieted to have a tiny glimpse into her life—the narrow hall with its clutter of coats and boots, the sound of a woman's voice. Her mother? Why did he care?

Perhaps because since he'd met her he'd viewed Hannah Stewart as nothing more than a means to his own end. First as his PA, efficient and capable, and now as his stand-in wife-to-be. Last night he'd realised that if this ridiculous charade was going to work, he needed to know more about Hannah. And he hadn't learned much, but what he had discovered was that getting to know Hannah even a little bit made him feel guilty for using her.

Sighing impatiently at his own pointless thoughts, Luca opened the door to the limo and stepped out into the street. It wasn't as if he was making Hannah's life difficult. She was getting a luxurious weekend on a Mediterranean island, all expenses paid. And if she had to play-act a bit, what was the big deal? He'd make it worth her while.

He pressed the doorbell, and Hannah answered the door almost immediately. She wore her usual work outfit of a dark pencil skirt and a pale silk blouse, this time grey and pink. Pearls at her throat and ears and low black heels complemented the outfit. There was nothing wrong with it, but it wasn't what his fiancée would be wearing to accompany him on a weekend house party. She looked like a PA, not a woman in love on a holiday.

'What happened to the outfits I bought you yesterday?' Luca demanded.

'Hello to you too,' Hannah answered. 'I'm saving them for when I'm actually on Santa Nicola.' She arched an eyebrow. 'Being on the aeroplane isn't part of the social occasion, is it?'

'Of course not.' Luca knew he couldn't actually fault Hannah. She was acting in accordance to the brief he had given her. He'd tell her the truth soon enough…when there was no chance of anything going wrong. Nothing could risk his plan for this weekend. 'Are you packed?'

'Of course.' She reached for her suitcase but Luca took it first. 'I'll put it in the boot.'

'Hello, Mr Moretti.' An older woman with faded eyes and grey, bobbed hair emerged from behind Hannah to give him a tentative smile.

'Good morning.' Belatedly Luca realised how snappish he must have sounded when talking to Hannah. This whole experience was making him lose his cool, his control. He forced as charming a smile as he could and extended his hand to the woman who took it.

'I'm Diane Stewart, Hannah's mother—'

'Lovely to meet you.'

'I should go, Mum,' Hannah said. She slipped on a black wool coat, lifting her neat ponytail away from the collar. Luca had a sudden, unsettling glimpse of the nape of her neck, the skin pale, the tiny hairs golden and curling.

'I'll say goodbye to Jamie for you,' Diane promised and Luca looked sharply at Hannah, who flushed.

Jamie—a boyfriend? Clearly someone close to her.

Although maybe Jamie was a girl's name. A friend? A sister?

'Thanks, Mum,' she muttered, and quickly hugged her mother before walking towards the limo.

Luca handed the suitcase to his driver before getting in the back with Hannah. She was sitting close to the window, her face turned towards the glass.

'Do you live with your mother?' he asked.

'No, she just stayed the night because I was so late getting home.'

'Why was she there at all?'

She gave him a quick, quelling look. 'She's visiting.'

Hannah Stewart seemed as private as he was. Luca settled back in the seat. 'I'm sorry if I've cut your visit short.' He paused. 'You could have told me she was visiting. I would have made allowances.'

Hannah's look of disbelief was rather eloquent. Luca felt a dart of annoyance, which was unreasonable since he knew he wouldn't have made allowances. He needed Hannah's attendance this weekend too much. Still he defended himself. 'I'm not that unreasonable an employer.'

'I never said you were.'

Which was true. But he felt nettled anyway, as if he'd done something wrong. It was that damned guilt, for tricking her into this. He didn't like lying. He'd always played a straight bat, prided himself on his plain dealing. He'd lived with too many lies to act otherwise. But this was different, this was decades-deep, right down to his soul, and his revenge on Andrew Tyson was far more important than his PA's tender feelings. Feeling better for that reminder, Luca reached for his smartphone and started scrolling through messages.

Hannah sat back in her seat, glad to have that awkward goodbye scene over with. Luca had been surprisingly curious about her life, and she'd thankfully managed to deflect his questions. She'd never told her boss about her son, and she wanted to keep it that way. She knew instinctively that Luca Moretti would not take kindly to his PA having such an obligation of responsibility, no matter what he said about allowances. She was fortunate that her mother lived nearby and had always been happy to help out. Without Diane's help, Hannah never would have been able to take the job as Luca Moretti's PA. She certainly wouldn't have been able to perform it with the same level of capability.

Now she tried to banish all the thoughts and worries that had kept her up last night as she'd wondered what she was getting into, and if she was doing the right thing in leaving her son for two days. She wanted to stop wondering if she was coming across as gauche as she felt, or why her normally taciturn boss was suddenly turning his narrow-eyed attention to her.

No, today she'd told herself she was going to simply enjoy everything that came her way, whether it was champagne and caviar or a first-class plane ticket. This was an adventure, and she'd got out of the habit of enjoying or even looking for adventures. Since she'd had Jamie her life had become predictable and safe, which wasn't a bad thing but sometimes it was boring. She realised she was actually looking forward to a little bit of a shake-up.

'You're smiling,' Luca observed and, startled, Hannah refocused her gaze on her boss. He'd been watching her, she realised with a lurch of alarm. Or maybe it was simply awareness that she felt. A tingling spread through her body as his gaze remained resting on her, his mahogany-brown eyes crinkled at the corners, a faint smile tugging at his own mobile mouth. He wore a navy blue suit she'd probably seen before, with a crisp white shirt and silver-grey tie. Standard business wear, elegant and expensive, the suit cut perfectly to his broad shoulders and trim hips. Why was she noticing it today? Why was she feeling so *aware*?

'I was just thinking about flying first class,' she said.

'Ah yes. Something else you haven't done before.'

'No, and I'm looking forward to it.' She smiled wryly. 'I'm sure it's same old, same old for you.'

'It's refreshing to see someone experience something for the first time.' His mouth curved in a deeper smile, the look in his eyes disconcertingly warm. 'Tickly or not.'

She lifted her chin, fighting a flush. 'I admit, I'm not very experienced in the ways of the world.'

'Why aren't you?'

'Maybe because I'm not a millionaire?' Hannah returned dryly. 'Most people don't travel first class, you know.'

'I'm well aware. But plenty of people have tasted champagne.' He cocked his head, his warm gaze turning thoughtful. 'You seem to have missed out a bit on life, Hannah.'

Which was all too perceptive of him. And even though she knew it was true, it still stung. 'I've been working,' she replied with a shrug. 'And I have responsibilities…' She left it at that but Luca's eyes had narrowed.

'What kind of responsibilities?'

'Family,' she hedged. 'Nothing that interferes with my work,' she defended and he nodded, hands spread palm upward.

'As well I know. I do appreciate you coming for the weekend.'

'I didn't think I really had much choice,' Hannah returned, then drew an even breath. 'Why don't you tell me more about this weekend? You said it was a social occasion? How so?'

The warmth left Luca's eyes and Hannah felt tension steal into his body even though he'd barely moved.

'Andrew Tyson is a family man,' he stated. 'Wife, two children, resorts dedicated to providing people with the ultimate family experience.'

'Yes, I did some research on them when I was booking your travel,' Hannah recalled. '"A Tyson Holiday is a memory for ever,"' she quoted and Luca grimaced.

'Right.'

'You don't like the idea?'

'Not particularly.'

She shouldn't have been surprised. Luca Moretti had never struck her as the wife-and-kids type, which was why she'd kept her own son secret from him. He was never short of female company, though, and none of them lasted very long. A week at the most. 'Why are you going after these resorts if you don't really like the idea behind them?'

'I don't make business decisions based on personal preferences,' Luca answered shortly. One hand closed in a fist on his powerful thigh and he straightened it out slowly, deliberately, his palm flat on his leg, his fingers, long and tapered, stretching towards his knee. 'I make business decisions based on what is financially sound and potentially profitable.'

'But Andrew Tyson only has a handful of resorts, doesn't he? The Santa Nicola resort, one on Tenerife, one on Kos, one on—'

'Sicily, and then a couple in the Caribbean. Yes.'

'It's small potatoes to a man like you,' Hannah pointed out. Luca had orchestrated multibillion-dollar deals all around the world. A couple of family resorts, especially ones that looked as if they needed a bit of updating, hardly seemed his sort of thing.

Luca shifted in his seat. 'As I told you before, the land alone makes this a lucrative deal.'

'Okay, but you still haven't told me why this is a social occasion.'

'Because Tyson wants it to be one. He's always espoused family values, and so he wants each potential owner to socialise with him and his family.'

'So chatting up little kids?' Hannah couldn't quite keep the note of amusement from her voice. 'It sounds like your worst nightmare.'

'His children are grown up,' Luca answered. 'The son is only a year younger than I am.'

'Do his children have children?'

'I have no idea.' Luca sounded eminently bored. 'Probably. The son is married.'

Hannah considered the implications of everything he'd just said. So she'd be socialising with Andrew Tyson and his family, chatting up his children and generally being friendly? She was starting to realise why Luca had wanted her to come along.

'So you want me to be your front man,' she said slowly.

Luca swivelled to face her. 'Excuse me?'

'To do the talking,' Hannah explained. 'Chatting to his wife and children while you get on with the business side of things. Right?'

He gave one terse nod. 'Right.'

She settled back in her seat. 'All right. I can do that.'

'Good,' Luca answered, and he turned back to his phone.

The VIP lounge at the airport fully lived up to Hannah's expectations. She enjoyed the plush seats, the complimentary mimosas and breakfast buffet, and when Luca suggested she take advantage of the adjoining spa and get a manicure and pedicure, she decided to go for it. Why not enjoy all the opportunities that were on offer? It wasn't as if she had many chances to relax in a spa.

By the time they boarded the plane she was feeling pleasantly relaxed; one of the spa attendants had given her a head and neck massage while her feet had been soaking.

It had felt lovely, as had Luca's look of blatant male appreciation when she'd emerged from the spa—the attendant had insisted on doing her hair and make-up as well.

'You look good,' he said in approval, and, while Hannah knew she shouldn't care what Luca thought of her looks, his masculine admiration spoke to the feminine heart of her.

'I think,' she told him as they took their seats in the plane's first-class section, 'I could get used to this.'

Luca's mouth quirked up at one corner. 'I'm sure you could.' He accepted two flutes of champagne from the airline steward and handed one to Hannah. 'And now you should get used to this.'

'Why are you so determined to have me become used to champagne?' Hannah asked as she took a sip. Second time round the bubbles didn't tickle her nose quite so much.

'Why not? You should enjoy all of these new experiences.'

'True,' Hannah answered. 'And since you said this was a social occasion, I might as well.' She took another sip of champagne. '*Are* we meant to be working during the flight?'

'No.'

'So why did you put me up in first class?'

'I wanted to watch you enjoy the experience.'

Hannah felt her stomach dip at this implication of his words, the intimacy of them. She was suddenly conscious of how this all seemed: the champagne flute dangling from her fingers, the cosy enclave of their first-class seats, and Luca Moretti lounging next to her, not taking his warm gaze from hers. She swallowed hard.

'Well, I am enjoying it,' she said, striving for normality. 'Thank you.' The last thing she needed was to start crushing on her boss. He'd probably find that amusing—or maybe offensive, and fire her. She handed her half-drunk champagne to the steward and buckled her seat belt. Time to get things back to the way they'd always been.

Luca must have been thinking along the same lines because he reached for the in-flight magazine as the plane took off, and then spent the rest of the four-hour flight looking over some paperwork. Hannah asked him once if he needed her to do anything, and he snapped at her that he didn't.

In fact, with each passing hour of the flight, he seemed to get more and more tense, his muscles taut, his eyes shadowed, his face grim. Hannah wondered what was going on, but she didn't dare ask.

She tried to watch a movie but her mind was pinging all over the place, and so she ended up simply staring out of the window at the azure sky, waiting for the minutes and hours to pass.

And then they did, and they landed on Santa Nicola, the Mediterranean glittering like a bright blue promise in the distance.

'Is someone meeting us at the airport?'

'Yes, one of Tyson's staff is picking us up.' Luca rose from his seat and shrugged into his suit jacket. 'Let me do the talking.'

Okay... 'I thought you wanted me to socialise.'

'I do. But not with the staff.'

Bewildered, Hannah stared at him, but Luca's deliberately bland expression gave nothing away. He held a hand out to her to help her from her seat, and after a second's hesitation she took it.

The feel of his warm, dry palm sliding across and then enfolding hers was a jolt to her system, like missing the last step in a staircase. Instinctively she started to withdraw her hand but Luca tightened his hands over hers and pulled her forward.

'Come on,' he murmured. 'People are waiting.'

With his hand still encasing hers she followed him out of the plane, blinking in the bright sunlight as she navigated the narrow steps down to the tarmac. She was just thinking that she wished she'd packed her sunglasses in her carry-on rather than her suitcase when she heard someone call a greeting to Luca and then felt his arm snake around her waist.

Hannah went rigid in shock at the feel of his fingers splayed on one hip, her other hip pressed against his thigh.

'Signor Moretti! We are so pleased to welcome you to Santa Nicola.' A tanned, friendly-looking man in khaki shorts and a red polo shirt with the Tyson logo on the breast pocket came striding towards them. 'And this is...?' he asked, glancing at Hannah with a smile.

'Hannah Stewart,' Luca filled in smoothly, his arm still firmly about her waist. 'My fiancée.'

CHAPTER FOUR

HANNAH STOOD BLINKING stupidly at the man who had come forward. He reached for her hand and numbly she gave it to him.

'Signorina Stewart. So pleased to meet you! Signor Moretti mentioned he was bringing his fiancée, and we look forward to getting to know you. I am Stefano, one of the members of Mr Tyson's staff.'

Hannah could only stare at Stefano, trying to find the brain cells to string two words together. The only word she could think of was the one Luca had used with such confident precision. *Fiancée.*

What on earth…?

'Hannah,' Luca murmured, and she felt the pressure of his hand on her waist, the warmth of his palm seeping through her skirt.

Still reeling, she forced a smile onto her face. 'Pleased to meet you, I'm sure.'

As soon as she said the words she wished she hadn't. Now she was complicit in this…whatever *this* was. A lie, obviously. A ruthless deception—and for what purpose? Why on earth would Luca pretend she was something she wasn't?

Because he was pretending he was something he wasn't.

The answer was so blindingly obvious Hannah couldn't

believe she hadn't twigged earlier. Andrew Tyson was a family man, and this weekend was meant to be a social occasion. *Of course.* Luca Moretti, the famous womaniser, needed a woman. A fiancée to show he was the kind of family man Tyson must want him to be. What other reason could he have possibly had for introducing her that way? For *lying*?

'Come this way,' Stefano said, beckoning towards the waiting open-topped Jeep emblazoned with the Tyson logo, a dolphin jumping in front of a sun. 'Mr Tyson's villa is only a few minutes away.'

Hannah walked like an automaton towards the Jeep, Luca next to her, his arm still around her. She wanted to shrug it off but she didn't think she'd be able to; his grip was like a vice. She tried to catch his eye but he was staring blandly ahead. Damn the man. What on earth was she supposed to do now?

They got in the back of the Jeep and Stefano hopped in the front. Hannah was barely aware of the gorgeous surroundings: mountains provided a stunning, jagged backdrop to lush greenery that framed both sides of the paved single-track road. She'd read that Santa Nicola was virtually unspoilt, save for the resort, and she could see it now in the jungle of bright flowers that gave way to superbly landscaped gardens and high walls of pink sandstone.

'Luca,' she muttered meaningfully, although she hardly knew where to begin, how to protest. 'You can't—'

'I already have,' he murmured as the Jeep came to a stop in front of a sprawling villa, its pale stone walls climbing with ivy and bougainvillea.

'I know,' Hannah snapped. 'And you shouldn't have—' She was prevented from saying anything more by Stefano coming around to open the door on her side and help her out onto the cobbled pavement.

'Mr Tyson looks forward to welcoming you properly

this evening, during the cocktail hour. In the meantime you can both rest and refresh yourselves.'

'Thank you,' Hannah muttered, although everything in her cried out to end this absurd charade. She was so angry and shocked she could barely manage to speak civilly to Stefano, who of course had no idea what was going on. *Yet.*

And Hannah wondered how on earth she could tell him, or anyone here, the truth. Luca had made it virtually impossible, and yet still she fantasised about coming clean and watching Luca Moretti get the send-up he undoubtedly deserved. How dare he put her in this position?

Stefano led them into the gracious entryway of the villa, a soaring foyer that made the most of the house's unparalleled view of the sea. Down a long terracotta-tiled corridor, and then through double louvred doors into a spacious and elegant bedroom, a massive king-sized bed its impressive centrepiece, the French windows opened to a private terrace that led to the beach, gauzy curtains blowing in the sea breeze.

'This is marvellous, thank you,' Luca said, shaking Stefano's hand, and with a murmured farewell Stefano closed the doors behind them, finally, thankfully, leaving them alone.

Hannah whirled around to face Luca, who stood in the centre of the bedroom, hands in the pockets of his trousers, a faint frown on his face as he surveyed the room with its elegant furnishings in cream and light green.

'How could you?' she gasped out. 'How *dare* you?'

Luca moved his gaze to her. He seemed utterly unmoved, without a shred of remorse or embarrassment. 'If you are referring to the way I introduced you—'

'Of *course* I'm referring to that!'

'It was necessary.' And he strolled over to the windows as if that was actually the end of the discussion.

Hannah stared at his broad back, watching as he closed

and fastened the windows. Finally she managed to say in what she hoped was a level, reasonable voice, 'Do you actually think this can work?'

Luca turned around to face her, eyebrows arrogantly raised. 'I don't embark on ventures that are doomed to failure.'

'I think you may be in for a new experience, then,' Hannah snapped.

'Why? Why shouldn't Andrew Tyson believe you're my fiancée?'

'Because I'm *not*—'

'Are you not suitable?' Luca steamrolled over her, his voice silky and yet underlaid with iron. 'Are you not pretty or smart or sophisticated enough?'

A hot flush broke out over Hannah's body as she glared at him. 'No, I'm not,' she answered flatly. 'As you well know. I hadn't even flown first class before today—or drunk champagne—' Suddenly the memory of him pressing the flute into her hands, smiling at her with such gentle amusement, was enough to make her burst into tears. She swallowed hard before continuing furiously, realisation ripping away any illusions she'd had left. 'So everything you've done has been to maintain this…this ridiculous façade.' She glanced down at her varnished nails, her hands curling instinctively into fists. 'The manicure and pedicure?' she spat. 'The hair and make-up…' She remembered the look of approval in his eyes. *You look good.* And she'd inwardly preened at his praise. 'You just wanted me to look the part.'

'Is that so objectionable?'

'This whole farce is objectionable! You *tricked* me.'

Luca sighed, as if she were being so very tedious by objecting. 'I'm asking for very little, Hannah.'

'Very little? You're asking me to lie to strangers. To pretend to—to be in love with you!' The words rang out, making her wince. She hadn't meant it quite like *that*, and yet…that was what he was asking. Wasn't it?

'I'm not asking anything of the kind,' Luca returned evenly. 'Although surely it wouldn't be too hard?'

Hannah recoiled, horrified at the implication. Did he think he was so desirable—or simply that she was so desperate? 'Yes, it would,' she said stiffly. 'Since in actuality I barely know you. Which was the point of the little "getting to know you" spiel last night at dinner, wasn't it?' She shook her head, disgusted with both him and herself. She'd known something was off, but how on earth could she have suspected this? 'Well, at least now you know I'm an only child. That's something, I suppose. Make sure to mention it during the cocktail hour.'

'You know me well enough,' Luca answered, his tone deliberately unruffled. 'You've worked for me for three years. In fact,' he continued, strolling towards her, 'you probably know me better than anyone else does.'

'I do?' She blinked at him, surprised and a little saddened by this admission. She'd known Luca was a solitary man, but surely he had closer people in his life than his PA. 'What about your family?'

'Not around.'

'Where—?'

'You're the only person who sees me every day, Hannah. Who knows my preferences, my foibles and quirks. Yes, I think you know me very well.'

'Yes, but you don't know *me*.' And she didn't care whether she knew him or not. She wouldn't want to play-act as his fiancée even if they'd been best friends. Which they were most decidedly not.

'I think I know you a little bit,' Luca said, a smile curving the sensuous mouth Hannah suddenly couldn't look away from.

'What? How?' He didn't know anything. 'You've never asked me anything about my life until last night.'

'Maybe I don't need to ask.'

'What are you saying?' He'd taken a step closer to her and her stomach writhed and leapt in response, as if she'd swallowed snakes. She pressed one hand to her middle, knowing the gesture to be revealing, and stood her ground even though she desperately wanted to take a step away from him.

Instead he took a step closer. 'Let's see,' he murmured, his voice a low hum that seemed to reverberate right through her bones. He was close enough so that she could inhale the cedarwood scent of his aftershave, see the muscles corded in his neck. Some time since entering the room he'd loosened his silver silk tie and undone the top two buttons of his shirt, so she could see the strong brown column of his throat, the dark hairs sprinkling his chest below. She jerked her gaze away from the sight.

'You don't know me,' she stated firmly. 'At all. Because if you did, you'd know I'd never agree to something like this.'

'Which is why I didn't ask you, so perhaps I do know you after all.'

'You don't,' she insisted. He was close enough to breathe in, to feel his heat. If she reached one hand out she could place a palm on his chest, feel the crisp cotton of his shirt, the steady thud of his heart, the flex of his powerful muscles…

Hannah drew her breath in sharply, horrified by the nature of her thoughts. What kind of sorcerer was Luca Moretti, to weave this spell over her so easily?

'I think I do,' Luca murmured. He stood right in front of her, his gaze roving over her, searching, finding, feeling as intimate as a caress. 'I know you drink your coffee with milk and two sugars, although you pretend you have it black.'

'What…?' Her breath came out in a rush. It was such a little thing, but he was right. She added the sugar when she was alone because she was self-conscious about taking it. Every working woman in London seemed to drink their coffee black and eat lettuce leaves for lunch.

Somehow she managed to rally. 'That's not very much,' she scoffed.

'I'm only beginning,' Luca answered. 'I know you look at travel blogs on your lunch break. I know you have an incredible work ethic but you seem embarrassed by it sometimes. I know you're determined to be cheerful but sometimes, when you think no one is looking, you seem sad.'

Hannah drew a deep breath, too shocked to respond or even to blush. How had he seen all these things? How did he *know*?

'And,' Luca finished softly as he turned away, 'I know there is someone in your life named Jamie whom you care about very much.'

She stiffened. 'Well done, Sherlock,' she managed. 'You're obviously very perceptive, but it doesn't change what I think—that this is wrong, and you never should have forced me into this position.'

Luca turned back to her, the warmth she'd just seen in his eyes evaporated, leaving only chilly darkness. 'How exactly,' he asked, his voice dangerously soft, 'did I force you?'

'It's not as if you gave me a choice,' Hannah exclaimed. 'Introducing me as your fiancée! What was I supposed to do, tell them you were a liar?'

He shrugged, the movement elegant, muscles rippling underneath his shirt. 'You could have done.' He lifted his gaze to hers, those dark, cold eyes so penetrating. 'Why didn't you?'

'Because…'

'Because?' Luca prompted softly.

'It would have been very awkward,' Hannah said. 'For both of us.'

'What's a little awkwardness?'

'You might have fired me—'

He arched an eyebrow. 'And be sued for sexual harassment?'

'I could already sue you for that,' Hannah dared to suggest. Luca's eyes narrowed.

'And then you really would lose your job, just as I would lose mine.'

She swallowed. 'You could have paid me off.'

The smile he gave her was cynical and hard. 'Is that what you're suggesting?'

'No.' Appalled, Hannah wondered how on earth they'd pursued this line of conversation. She wasn't going to sue him, even if part of her inwardly railed that she should, that Luca Moretti deserved everything he had coming to him, including a whole lot of *awkwardness*.

'I don't want money,' she informed him stiffly. 'I simply don't want to be in this position, and I resent that you put me in it. Why didn't you tell me before?'

'Because you would have refused.'

She stared at his calm expression, his hard eyes. He stood before her, arrogant and assured, utterly unrepentant. 'You don't have a shred of remorse, do you?' she asked wonderingly.

'No,' Luca agreed, 'I don't. Because if you let go of your huffy indignation for a moment, Hannah, you'll realise I'm not asking very much of you.'

'You're asking me to lie.'

'And you've never lied before?'

She bit her lip. 'Of course, everyone's lied, but this is different—'

'Andrew Tyson is putting unreasonable expectations on the real-estate developer who buys his precious resorts,' Luca cut across her flatly. 'I *know* I'm the best man for the job, and I shouldn't have to be married to be selected. The injustice is his, not mine.'

'How many other developers are bidding on it?'

'Two, and they're both married.'

Somehow she found the temerity to joke. 'You weren't tempted to say I was your wife?'

'I was tempted,' Luca admitted. 'But I figured that would be too hard to pull off.'

'How pragmatic of you,' Hannah murmured. Her mind was still spinning but some of her self-righteous fury had deflated. She didn't know whether it was simply the awesome force of Luca's personality or because she actually sympathised with him a little. Or maybe it was because she was just too tired to keep it up.

Slowly she walked to a cream divan positioned in an alcove and sank onto its soft seat. 'So how do you propose—no pun intended—to make this work? Not,' she informed him with swift asperity, 'that I'm actually thinking of going along with this idea.'

'Of course not,' Luca murmured. Hannah watched, mesmerised, as he tugged off his tie and then began to unbutton his shirt.

'What are you doing?' she squeaked.

'Changing. We're due for cocktails in less than an hour.'

'Can't you use the bathroom?' She nodded towards the door that led to what looked like a sumptuous en suite.

'Why should I?' Luca's smile was wicked. 'We're engaged to be married, after all.'

'You're impossible.' Hannah closed her eyes against the sight of Luca shrugging off his shirt. Even so she'd had a glimpse of bronzed, burnished skin, rippling muscles, and crisp, dark hair that veed down to the waistband of his trousers.

'You're not the first person to say so,' Luca answered. She could hear him undressing and even with her eyes closed she could imagine it, picture him kicking off his trousers, revealing long, muscular legs, wearing nothing but a pair of boxer shorts, perhaps in navy satin…

Good grief, but she needed to get a grip. Hannah took a deep breath. 'So you still haven't told me how this is going to work.'

'We're going to act like we're engaged. Simple.'

'Simple?' She opened her eyes to glare at Luca; he stood across the room, buckling the belt on a pair of grey trousers. His chest was still gloriously bare. 'It's not simple, Luca. We're not engaged. We barely know each other. If someone asks either one of us anything about our relationship or how we met, we'll have no idea what to say.'

'It's best to keep as close to the truth as possible,' Luca advised as he reached for a light blue shirt and shrugged into it. 'You're still my PA.'

'And we just happen to be engaged. Convenient.'

He shot her a quick, hard smile. 'It is, isn't it? Now you should get ready. We're due to meet Tyson for cocktails shortly.'

CHAPTER FIVE

LUCA STARED OUT at the setting sun turning the placid sea to gold and waited for Hannah to emerge from the bathroom. He tried to ignore the guilt that flickered through him, an unpleasant ripple of sensation. All right, so he'd tricked her. He shouldn't have. But he hadn't had any choice. Not that Hannah would be able to understand that, and he had no intention of explaining it to her. She didn't seem to be quite so angry now, although she had shut the door rather firmly after flouncing in there to get changed.

Sighing restlessly, Luca turned away from the spectacular view. Every nerve ending tingled with anticipation at coming face to face with Andrew Tyson. In the three months since Tyson had announced he was selling his chain of family resorts, Luca hadn't actually spoken to the man, not even on the telephone. Everything had been done through intermediaries, until this weekend. Until now, when he would finally look upon the man he'd hated for so long. He *had* to close this deal. And he'd do whatever it took to accomplish that.

'Are you ready?' he called to Hannah. They were due on the terrace for drinks in five minutes.

'Yes.' She unlocked and opened the door, emerging from the bathroom with her head held high even as uncertainty flickered in her eyes. Luca felt the breath rush from his lungs as he took in her appearance.

She wore a cocktail dress in plum-coloured silk; the pure, clean line of the material across her collarbone drew his attention to the elegance of her shoulders and neck as well as the slight, enticing curve of her breasts. The dress fitted perfectly to her tiny waist and then flared out around her thighs, ending at her knees. Her long, shapely legs were encased in sheer stockings and she'd worn her hair not in its usual neat ponytail, but in loose waves about her face. She looked clean and fresh and utterly alluring.

Luca finally found his voice. 'You look…good.'

'I meet with your approval?' Hannah surmised tartly. 'Well, I need to look the part, don't I?' She went over to her suitcase and riffled through her belongings. 'I don't feel at all guilty for letting you buy me a fortune in clothes, by the way.'

'And so you shouldn't.' The rays of the setting sun caught the golden glints in her hair. Luca watched as she moved her hair over to one shoulder in order to put on her earrings. He found something almost unbearably erotic about watching her do this, her neck exposed, her slender hands fitting the earring into her ear. Her feet, he saw, were bare.

'I suppose I'll have to give them back when this charade is over?' she asked as she reached for a pearl necklace.

'No, not at all. You may keep them. They're yours.'

She fiddled with the necklace, unable to do the clasp, and Luca walked towards her. 'Here, let me.' His fingers brushed her nape as he did the clasp and he felt a shudder go through her. Felt it go through himself. He couldn't resist brushing his fingers against that tender, silky skin one more time before he stepped away.

'Thank you,' she murmured, not looking at him. He could see a rosy flush spreading across the creamy skin of her throat and face.

'I should have bought you some appropriate jewellery.'

'I think that would be going above and beyond,' she answered lightly. 'Pearls surely suffice.'

'Yes…but I'd like to see you with diamonds. And sapphires. They'd look lovely against your pale skin.'

She dipped her head, hiding her expression. 'Thank you.'

Luca watched her, wishing he had a reason to touch her again. 'You don't seem as angry as you were before.'

She glanced quickly at him before lowering her lashes. 'I suppose I'm not. The truth is, I actually do like you, Mr—'

'Surely now is the time to call me Luca.'

'Luca. Sorry, old habits die hard, I suppose.' She sighed and then straightened before moving away from him. 'I'd better not slip up with that one, huh? Anyway.' She reached for a wrap in matching plum-coloured lace; it looked as fragile and delicate as cobwebs. 'I like working for you, even if I resent having to participate in this farce of an engagement. I don't want you to lose face or your job, and I certainly don't want to lose mine. So.' She turned to him, a determined smile on her face. 'Here we are.'

'Here we are.' He gazed at her and she gazed back, and the moment stretched and spun out while the sun continued to set and the room became dark with shadows.

Eventually, Luca didn't know how long it took, he roused himself and reached for her hand. 'We should go.'

'All right.'

And with her fingers loosely threaded through his, he led her out of the room.

The terrace was bathed with the last rays of the setting sun as Luca led her through the open French windows and out onto the smooth paving stones. Torches flickered in the deepening twilight and couples milled around along with several staff members proffering trays of champagne and frothy-looking cocktails.

Smiling wryly to herself, Hannah took a flute of champagne with murmured thanks. She took a sip, enjoying the crisp bubbles bursting on her tongue, and gazed around at the assortment of people. There were two other couples, an urbane, blond man with a tall, bony-looking woman who Hannah vaguely recognised, and a middle-aged man with greying hair and a smiling wife who had squeezed herself into a dress of green satin. Their host, as far as she could tell, was nowhere to be seen.

Next to her Luca looked relaxed and faintly amused, but Hannah could feel the tension emanating from him. The fingers that clasped his flute of champagne were white-knuckled. She wondered again why he cared so much, and knew he would never tell her. And she would probably never work up the courage to ask.

'Greetings!' A jovial-looking man in his seventies appeared in the French windows, rubbing his hands and smiling in expectation. Hannah recognised Andrew Tyson from the photograph she'd seen on the Tyson Resorts website. Genial, running slightly to fat, with sandy silvery hair and deep-set brown eyes. In his youth he must have been quite handsome. He still possessed a vigorous charisma now.

'I'm so pleased to have you here at last,' he said as he strolled onto the terrace. 'Luca, James, and Simon. You all know each other?'

The men exchanged quick glances and terse nods. 'Excellent, excellent. And you all have drinks?' His gaze moved over the crowd to rest on Luca.

'Luca Moretti,' he said as if accessing a mental Rolodex. 'We've never actually met, but I have, of course, heard of your many accomplishments in the world of real estate.'

Hannah glanced at Luca and saw his expression was bland. 'Thank you,' he murmured.

'And you are recently engaged?' Andrew's gaze sharpened, his smile turning almost sly. 'For I've heard of your accomplishments elsewhere.'

Luca drew Hannah forward, as if displaying a trophy. She tried to smile even though she didn't like being pushed forward as if for inspection. 'Indeed. Please meet my wife-to-be, Hannah Stewart.'

'Hannah.' Tyson glanced at her appraisingly, and for one horrible second Hannah wondered if he would see through this whole ridiculous charade. And she realised she didn't want to be exposed in such a way, and she didn't want Luca to be exposed. He might have lied and tricked her terribly, but now that she was embroiled in this ploy she wanted it to succeed.

'I'm very pleased to meet you,' she told Tyson, and stuck out her hand for him to shake. He kissed it instead, his lips a little damp, and next to her Luca shifted restlessly.

'Likewise, of course,' Tyson said. 'Now how did the two of you meet?'

'Hannah is my PA,' Luca intervened swiftly. 'We met at work. I'm not one to advocate mixing business with pleasure, but in this instance it was impossible not to.' He sent Hannah a lingering, loving glance that didn't quite meet his eyes. Still she felt herself tingle. Her body was reacting to Luca's, or maybe it was her mind reacting to his words. She knew them to be lies but they affected her anyway. It had been a long time since she'd been complimented by a man in any shape or form.

'I can see why,' Andrew said with a charmingly flirtatious smile for her. 'How did he propose, Hannah? If you don't mind me asking?'

Uh-oh. Her mind blanked for one awful second before she thought *screw it* and gave a light, teasing laugh. 'Oh, it was so romantic, wasn't it, Luca?' she practically purred, sliding an arm around her intended's waist. His body tensed under her hand and she enjoyed the feel of bunched muscle and taut abs before she continued with her story. 'He surprised me with a trip to Paris for the weekend—on a private jet.' She slid Luca what she hoped was an adoring look from under her lashes, enjoying the way his wary expression changed to one of cautious interest. He wanted to know where she was going with this. 'And then one magical evening he took me to the top of the Eiffel Tower—he'd rented the whole thing out so it was completely private.'

'I didn't think you could rent the Eiffel Tower,' Andrew said and Hannah continued without missing a beat.

'Oh, you can, if you know the right people.' She dared to wink. 'Isn't that right, Luca?'

He smiled blandly. 'It is.'

'And then what happened?' The woman in green satin had asked. Everyone was listening to her story now, clearly intrigued by the over-the-top romanticism. Hannah knew she shouldn't lay it on too thick; this was Luca Moretti, after all, and his reputation had clearly preceded him. And yet…if Luca was going to do a thing, she knew he'd do it properly, proposing marriage included.

'And then he told me how madly in love he was with me,' she finished blithely, 'and he proposed. Down on one knee.' She ended this utter fabrication with a happy sigh.

Andrew Tyson smiled faintly as he nodded towards her hand. 'But you don't have a ring, my dear.'

'Oh, but I do,' Hannah assured him. 'Luca presented me with the most magnificent ring—a family heirloom, actually, hundreds of years old, although he changed the design for me. Sapphires and diamonds,' she added, remembering what Luca had said earlier. 'Gorgeous.' She paused for a moment, picturing the fictitious ring, while everyone remained silent and spellbound.

'What happened to it, then?' asked the lanky woman rather sulkily.

'Oh, it was too big. Silly Luca.' She patted him playfully on the cheek and ignored the glimmer of warning in his mahogany eyes. 'It's at the jeweller's being resized.' She turned a twinkling smile onto Andrew Tyson. 'But I assure you, the next time I see you, you'll be suitably blinded.' Now *why* had she said that? She didn't want to see Andrew Tyson again. She certainly didn't want to keep up this pretence. She'd just got carried away.

'I'm sure,' Andrew murmured. 'Charmed, my dear, charmed.' He turned to another guest and Hannah only just kept from sagging with relief, now that the adrenaline was leaving her in a cold rush. She could feel the watchful gazes of the other businessmen and their wives, no doubt wondering what a man like Luca Moretti saw in her.

'You're a natural,' Luca murmured in her ear. 'You should be on the stage.'

'Shh,' Hannah chided. They eased away from the group as they both gazed out at the sea, now swathed in darkness. The moon was just rising, sending a sheen of silver over the water. 'Actually, I quite enjoyed myself.'

'I could tell.' He shot her an amused look, although Hannah could still feel how tense he was. 'You almost had me believing I gave you an heirloom ring.'

'Well, that's the point, isn't it?' Hannah replied. Actually, she had enjoyed believing in the fantasy for a few moments. Wearing the dress, drinking the champagne, acting as if a gorgeous, powerful man adored her. It could get addictive, enjoying all this attention and luxury, and she needed to remember none of this was real.

'If I'd known how much you'd get into the spirit of the thing,' Luca remarked, 'I would have let you in on the secret earlier.'

'I think it's more of a case of needs must,' Hannah returned. She glanced back at the assembled group. 'We should mingle, I suppose.'

'I suppose.'

'Tyson's wife isn't here? Or his children?'

The traces of amusement on Luca's face disappeared. 'They're joining him tomorrow. Tomorrow's dinner will be the big black-tie event.'

'When will he announce who has won the bid?'

Luca shrugged. 'Who knows? I think he's toying with all of us.'

Hannah glanced at Andrew, who was working his way through the crowd, talking to everyone individually. 'He seems a nice man.'

'Appearances can be deceiving.'

She turned back to Luca, surprised by the hardness in his voice. 'You don't like him.'

'I don't know the man,' Luca answered as he tossed back the rest of his drink. 'But I don't like being forced into play-acting. His demands are unreasonable and irrelevant.'

'And yet you still chose to go after his resorts.'

'I told you twice now, the land is valuable. Now let's go.' He took her arm and moved back to the crowd, and Hannah had no choice but to follow his lead. The Luca Moretti she knew wouldn't kowtow to anyone's demands, especially if he thought they were unreasonable. So why was he in this case?

She had no time to ponder the question as they were plunged back into the complicated social dynamics of three men who clearly respected if not liked each other, and were all bidding for the same job, while Andrew Tyson presided over them all.

At dinner Hannah sat next to Daniela, the sulky, beautiful woman who was partner to James, the CEO of a slick development company in the City. 'So how long have you been working for Luca?' she asked Hannah as the first course was served.

Luca, was it? Hannah covertly studied Daniela's tall,

lithe build, the long blond hair she kept tossing over her shoulder in an artful, deliberate way. 'Three years.'

'And you have been engaged for how long?'

A couple of hours. 'A few weeks.' Hannah took a sip of the cold cucumber soup to keep from having to say anything else.

'I never thought a man like Luca would marry,' Daniela said with a burning stare for the man in question, who was chatting with Simon, the third developer, across the table. 'He always seemed like the type to love and leave.'

'Until he found someone he wanted to stay with,' Hannah returned.

Daniela arched an eyebrow, the scepticism evident on her face. 'You're quite different from the women Luca is usually seen with. Not quite as...polished.'

Stung by this unsubtle put-down, Hannah lifted her chin. 'I didn't realise you knew him.'

'Oh, I know him,' Daniela said darkly and Hannah inwardly seethed. Luca could have warned her that a former paramour would be here, unsheathing her claws and trying to draw blood. And what if she gave something away to this elegant harpy? Daniela might know more about Luca than she did. Judging by her smouldering looks, it seemed almost a certainty. The idea made her feel unsettled in a way she didn't like. She wasn't *jealous*, just annoyed and angry all over again at Luca putting her in this position.

By the time the dessert plates had been cleared and coffee served, Hannah was having trouble keeping up her sparkly pretence. The excitement of pretending to be someone she wasn't had worn thin, and she longed only to return to their room and go to sleep. Actually, what she really wanted to do was go back to London and snuggle with her son. When she'd been in the bathroom changing she'd managed to speak to Jamie on the phone for a few minutes, listening to him chatter about his day, but it wasn't enough. It was never enough.

Luca must have seen the slump of her shoulders or the fatigue on her face for in one graceful movement he rose from the table. 'It's been a lovely evening, but I fear I've tired my fiancée out. Do you mind if we excuse ourselves?'

'Not at all, not at all,' Andrew replied as he also rose. 'We'll see you both in the morning.'

Luca and Hannah made their farewells to the rest of the group and then they walked in silence to their bedroom; with each step Hannah was remembering that big bed and how small it now actually seemed. They surely wouldn't share it. Luca would be a gentleman and make up a bed on the divan. Or so she hoped.

And yet even the thought of sharing the same room with Luca made her head go light and her palms turn damp. He was so *male*, so potently virile and sexual. She'd been immune—mostly—in their usual office environment, but she felt it keenly here, when they were sharing a bedroom and the moonlight and the gentle whooshing of the sea conspired to make everything seem romantic.

Luca opened the door to their bedroom, stepping aside so Hannah could go in first. He shrugged off his jacket while Hannah kicked off her heels with a groan. 'Wretched things.'

'You're not a fan of high heels?'

'I like taking them off.' The room was bathed in moonlight, the windows open to the sea breeze, the light from the lamps on the bedside tables giving out a cosy glow. Hannah glanced at the bed, which had been turned down, the cream duvet folded back to reveal the silky sheet beneath. A heart-shaped chocolate in gold foil nestled on each pillow. 'How is that going to work?' she asked, deciding to tackle the problem head-on.

Luca barely glanced at the bed. 'How is what going

to work?' His fingers had already gone to the buttons of his shirt, and, heaven help her, he was going to take it off again. And this time she might let herself watch.

'Sleeping arrangements,' Hannah said, dragging her gaze away from the tantalising glimpse of Luca's chest. 'We can't both sleep in the bed.'

'Oh?' He sounded amused. 'Why can't we?'

'Because!' Startled, she turned back to him and watched as he shrugged out of his shirt and then went for his belt buckle. '*Luca.* Can't you change in the bathroom?'

'What are you, a nun? If it makes you feel better, I won't sleep in the nude as I usually do.'

'What a prince,' Hannah gritted through her teeth. 'Seriously, Luca—'

'Seriously,' he said as he reached for a pair of drawstring pyjama pants that were going to leave very little to the imagination. 'It's a bed. It's huge. We can both sleep in it. I need my sleep, and I don't want anyone suspecting that we're not sleeping together. And, in case you're worried, I'm perfectly capable of sharing a bed without ravishing the other occupant.'

Hannah swung away as Luca dropped his trousers to change into his pyjamas. 'I'm not afraid of that,' she said, staring hard at the curtains drawn against the French windows. She could hear the whisper of fabric over Luca's legs, imagined his powerful thighs, muscles flexing...

Stop. Hannah pressed one hand to her flaming cheek. She really had to get a grip on her imagination. *And* her hormones.

'I'm dressed,' he said mildly. 'You can turn around.'

Taking a deep breath, Hannah did so. And dropped her gaze to his bare chest, his perfectly sculpted pectoral muscles lightly dusted with dark hair. The pyjama bottoms were slung low on his hips, so she could see the taut muscles of his abdomen, tapering down to… Quickly she jerked her gaze back up.

'If you're not worried that I'm going to ravish you, what are you afraid of?' Luca asked.

Why did he have to sound so reasonable? And make her feel so ridiculous? 'It just doesn't seem appropriate,' Hannah muttered.

'Hannah, we passed "appropriate" a while ago.' He took a step towards her, his hands outstretched. 'Look, you were magnificent back there. The whole thing about the Eiffel tower and the ring? I was practically believing it myself. And you seemed like you were having fun.' Hannah looked away, biting her lip. 'Well?' Luca pressed. 'Were you?'

'Sort of,' she admitted. What woman wouldn't like to step into a fairy tale for an evening, even if it was fake?

'So maybe you should let go of what's appropriate in this situation,' Luca suggested, his voice dropping to a beguiling murmur, standing only a step away from her.

She had the insane urge to reach out and *stroke* his chest.

'Let yourself enter into the spirit of the thing,' Luca continued, his voice all honeyed persuasion. 'Like you did tonight.'

'And share your bed.'

'In the literal sense only.'

'Oh, you know I didn't mean *that*,' Hannah protested, her face flaming once more. She shook her head. 'Honestly, you're incorrigible.'

'You've only just realised that?' He turned to the huge bed and plucked the chocolate from the pillow. 'So what are you waiting for?' he asked as he unwrapped the chocolate and popped it into his mouth. 'Come to bed.'

CHAPTER SIX

LUCA LAY IN BED, his arms braced behind his head, as he waited for Hannah to emerge from the bathroom. She'd been in there for quite a while, no doubt summoning her nerve to come out.

He didn't feel bad about sharing the bed with her. He'd even suggested, before she'd huffed into the bathroom clutching her pyjamas, that she was free to construct a barrier of pillows between them if she really did fear for her virtue.

She'd rolled her eyes. 'I can handle it,' she'd retorted, which amused him because she'd been the one to get all worked up about the issue in the first place.

She'd been incredible tonight, though. Sparkling and funny and charming, and he'd seen how Andrew Tyson had come under her spell. *He* almost had. Luca had found his gaze continually moving towards her, ensnared by her tinkling laugh, her teasing smile, the way the light caught the honeyed highlights in her hair.

Several times he'd leaned forward to try to catch what she was saying, needing to know and not because of the pretence. Because he really wanted to hear.

Then he'd reminded himself that she was playing a part and so was he, and Andrew Tyson was falling for it. That was all that mattered. He had no sympathy for the man, no pity whatsoever. Watching Tyson, Luca had barely been able to sit across from him and keep a smile on his face. Hannah had at least provided a distraction from the rage that simmered beneath the surface, threatening to bubble over.

The door to the bathroom opened and Hannah stepped out. Her hair was loose about her face and she wore…

'What the hell is that?'

Hannah glanced down at her roomy, faded T-shirt and shapeless boxer shorts. 'My pyjamas.'

'Didn't you get pyjamas at the boutique?'

'If you mean the scrap of lace that barely passes for a negligee, then yes. But I am not wearing that.' She glowered at him, a flush firing her face. 'There are limits, Luca.'

'You can't wear those. The staff come in to serve us breakfast in bed in the morning.'

Hannah didn't look at him as she crossed the room and climbed into bed, dragging the duvet up to her chin. 'So?'

'So,' Luca answered, 'I want them thinking that we spent the night ravishing each other as any newly engaged couple on holiday would.'

The minute he said the words images emblazoned themselves on his brain. Heat flared inside him. And he felt Hannah stiffen next to him.

'And they won't think of that if I'm dressed like this?' Hannah said after a moment. Her voice sounded suffocated. 'Too bad.'

She turned away from him, her body radiating tension. Luca sighed and snapped off the lights. He'd pushed it far enough, he supposed, although in truth he wanted to see Hannah in a sexy nightgown for his own sake, never mind the staff who would come in the next morning.

'You could have warned me about your friend,' Hannah said after a tense silence when Luca had been willing the desire coursing through his body to fade.

'My friend?' he asked, nonplussed.

'Daniela. She obviously knows you.'

'We've met.'

'You mean you've slept with her.'

Luca was silent, considering the assumption. He hadn't slept with Daniela, although the Russian model had made it clear she'd wanted to. And considering what he was asking Hannah to do, he supposed she deserved to know the truth. 'We went on a date,' he said. 'About a year ago. But nothing happened.'

'I suppose she wished something did.' Her voice was slightly muffled.

'Maybe,' Luca allowed.

'Judging by the burning looks she was giving you over dinner, I'd say definitely. And she wasn't impressed with me either. Not like that's too surprising, though.'

Hannah's words ended on a sigh and surprise flickered through him. 'Why do you say that?' he asked quietly.

Hannah didn't answer for a moment. In the darkness he couldn't see her features, only the taut shape of her body under the duvet. He heard the soft draw of her breath and it felt weirdly intimate. He realised he'd never actually slept in the same bed with a woman before. His assignations—he couldn't even call them relationships—had always ended with a definitive post-coital farewell.

'Well,' Hannah said at last, 'it's obvious, isn't it? A Plain Jane PA is hardly your type.'

'You're not a Plain Jane, Hannah.'

She laughed, a snort of genuine amusement that made him smile. 'Come on, Luca. Your normal type is supermodels and socialites, right? I'm neither.'

'That doesn't mean you're plain.'

'I'm not glamorous or gorgeous,' she returned. 'I don't

mind.' She shifted where she lay, so he felt the mattress dip beneath them. 'Why do you date socialites and supermodels? I mean, why not a normal woman?'

'Well.' Luca cleared his throat, caught between amusement and a surprising embarrassment. 'I'm not really interested in their personalities.'

Hannah was silent for a moment. 'Well, that's blunt,' she said at last.

'I try to be honest.'

'Except when you're duping a houseful of people into believing you're about to be married.' She rolled over so she was turned towards him, although Luca couldn't actually see her face in the darkness. He had the alarming impulse to reach out to her, curve a hand around her neck and draw her closer. Kiss those lush lips he'd found himself sneaking looks at all evening. 'Why do you go for shallow?' she asked. 'Why is it just sex for you? Because that's what you're saying, isn't it?'

Luca was silent for a long moment, struggling to form an answer that was honest without being too revealing. 'Because it isn't worth it,' he finally said. 'To have more.'

He waited for Hannah's response, his body tensing against the possible onslaught of questions. Her voice came out in a soft, sorrowful sigh.

'Maybe it isn't,' she agreed quietly.

Luca waited for her to say more but she didn't. He closed his eyes, telling himself it was better that way, because he didn't want to explain his answer even if part of him wanted to know why Hannah agreed with him.

With his eyes closed, his other senses were heightened, so he could breathe in her light floral scent, feel the warmth of her body so close to his, hear the gentle draw and sigh of her breathing.

Desire flared through him again and more intensely this time, and ruefully Luca acknowledged that he might be the one in need of a pillow barrier. He rolled onto his other side, away from Hannah, and tried to will himself to sleep.

If this were a romcom, Hannah thought wryly, she and Luca would fall asleep and then somehow, in the night, they would wake tangled up in each other's arms. They'd gaze into each other's eyes, still caught in the throes of sleep, and then Luca would brush a kiss across her lips, slide his hand down her body, everything fogged with sleep…

Hannah realised her rueful imagination was fast turning into fantasy, and heat flooded her belly at just the thought of Luca looking at her that way. Touching her that way.

She squeezed her eyes shut, trying to banish the images. Maybe her mother was right, and she needed to start dating again. Diane was always worried that Hannah worked too much, that she didn't have a social life of her own. Hannah replied that she didn't have the time for a social life, but the truth was relationships were too much risk. Maybe that was something she and Luca had in common.

She sighed, the sound loud in the stillness of the room.

'Problem?' Luca asked, his voice sounding strained.

'This is a bit awkward,' Hannah said into the darkness.

'Just go to sleep, Hannah.' Luca sounded annoyed now, and, chastised, Hannah rolled away from him. She could do this. She was exhausted, for heaven's sake. She needed her sleep. Yet all she could think about, all she could focus on, was Luca's body a few feet from hers. Maybe only a foot. And his chest was bare. She imagined resting her cheek against it, her arms around his waist, their legs tangled together.

She stifled a groan. It was going to be a very long night.

Hannah woke to a light knock on the door and she blinked blearily as she raised her head from the pillow.

'Just a moment,' Luca called, and then his arm snaked out, hooking around her waist, and drawing her towards the hard wall of the chest. The feel of his body coming into full, intimate contact with hers stole the breath from her lungs and she froze in shock. Then she felt his obvious arousal nudging her thighs and she gasped aloud.

'It's morning,' Luca muttered. 'That's all it is.'

All right, fine. She was a grown-up; she understood basic biological functions. But *honestly.* This was way, way past the call of duty. And yet it felt so very nice.

As the door opened, Hannah adjusted to the feel of Luca's body against her own. This was what she had fantasised about last night, and the reality felt even better than she had imagined. His chest was warm and solid and the smell of him was intoxicating, overwhelming. The press of his hand on her lower back made her rock helplessly into his hips, his erection settling between her thighs, making heat flare sharply inside her. Luca's breath hissed between his teeth as his body instinctively pushed back before he stilled.

'Hannah.'

Mortified, she tried to move away, but Luca's arms were like steel bands around her. 'Stay still,' he commanded in a low voice that was as hard as iron.

Two staff members wheeled in a cart laden with two breakfast trays, and Luca eased up in bed, taking Hannah with him so they were both reclining against the pillows, the duvet pulled demurely across their laps. Hannah wished, bizarrely perhaps, that she were wearing the gorgeous lace negligee, revealing as it was. She felt ridiculous in her oversized T-shirt that had faded to an unappealing grey colour from too many washes. And her hair… She lifted her hands to the tangle around her face and Luca smiled at her, tucking a stray strand behind her ear.

'Nothing like a little bedhead in the morning,' he said

with a teasing smile, and Hannah blinked, discomfited, until she realised he was putting on a show for the staff.

'I'm glad you love me no matter what I look like,' she replied sweetly. 'Or what I wear.'

The staff handed them their trays and with murmured thanks Hannah sat up straighter, taking in the freshly squeezed orange juice, the carafe of coffee, toast and fresh fruit and the most delicious-looking omelette. She could definitely get used to this.

The members of staff left quietly and Hannah reached for a piece of toast. She was not going to look at Luca, and remember how it had felt to have his arms around her, to arch into him… *What* had possessed her to do that?

'So what's the plan for today?' she asked, deciding that ignoring that whole brief interlude was the best way to go. Luca, it seemed, did not agree.

'Just to be clear,' he said flatly, 'we're going to keep this as play-acting, and nothing more.'

Hannah eyed him resentfully, trying to keep the hot tide of embarrassment at bay. 'You're the one who insisted we share a bed.'

'You're the one who rocked against me like a wanton,' Luca snapped.

'A wanton?' Hannah pushed aside the breakfast tray, her appetite having vanished, and scrambled out of the bed. 'What century do you live in?'

'I mean it, Hannah—'

'Trust me, I take the warning. And just like you, Luca Moretti, I am perfectly able to sleep in the same bed as someone without ravishing them!' Caught between fury, mortification, and tears, she grabbed her clothes and slammed into the bathroom.

Luca sighed and closed his eyes as the slam of the bathroom door echoed through the room. He'd handled that about as badly as possible. Calling Hannah Stewart a wanton was like calling Andrew Tyson a saint. Absurd. Laughable, except there was nothing remotely funny about either situation.

He opened his eyes and raked a hand through his hair, wondering how best to do damage control. Honesty? The truth was, he'd been far more aroused and tempted by Hannah's slender body than he'd any right to be. When she'd rocked into him he'd felt his precious control starting to disintegrate, and it had taken its last shreds to keep from shouting at the staff to leave them alone so he could bury himself deep in her willing body. *He* was the wanton, not Hannah.

He had no idea why his pretty enough PA affected him this way; perhaps it was simply the strangeness of the situation, or that his senses and emotions felt raw from facing Tyson again after so many years. He couldn't deny it, though; he'd been fighting an unreasonable and most inconvenient attraction to her since this whole charade had begun.

He drank his coffee, musing on the unwelcome distraction of his surprisingly delectable PA. He needed to focus on the real reason he'd come to Santa Nicola. He couldn't let anything distract him from his purpose. Having Hannah upset or embarrassed was just as difficult and distracting as having them both fighting—and flirting with—a sexual attraction he didn't think either of them had expected. It was time to nip this in the bud.

Fifteen minutes later Hannah emerged from the bathroom, her hair damp, her face composed. She wore a pretty pink linen sundress that skimmed her breasts and hugged her slim waist. She didn't so much as look at Luca.

'I'm sorry,' Luca said as he pushed his breakfast tray away. 'I shouldn't have said that.'

'You do have a tendency towards bluntness,' Hannah

replied as she struggled to put on her pearl necklace. This time Luca didn't offer to help.

'I wasn't being blunt,' he said. 'I was dissembling.'

She glanced at him and then quickly away again. 'How so?'

'I'm attracted to you,' he stated flatly. 'To my own surprise.'

'I thought it was just the morning,' she returned tartly, but he could see her cheeks pinken.

'It was more than the morning,' Luca admitted gruffly. 'I was angry at myself, and my body's reaction, rather than at you.'

'It must be terribly irritating to be attracted to someone like me,' Hannah agreed. Luca realised that underneath her embarrassment, she was blisteringly angry. 'Someone with feelings and a normal bra size.'

'Hannah,' he warned through gritted teeth. The last thing he needed this morning was a big, messy row with the woman who was supposed to be his compliant, biddable faux fiancée.

'Luca,' Hannah returned mockingly. She whirled around, her colour high, her golden-brown eyes blazing. 'How about you listen to me for a change? I didn't ask to come to this island. I didn't ask to pretend to be your fiancée. I didn't ask to share your bed! In fact, at every step, I've asked for the opposite. I've wanted more space, not less. And then you have the audacity, the wretched nerve, to call me a wanton!'

'I told you why—'

'And you think that makes it better? You said it like you couldn't even understand why you were attracted to someone like me. *To my surprise.* Well, thanks for that, Luca. Thanks very much.' She turned away again, her hands shaking as she reached for her pearl earrings.

All right, he could see how what he'd said might have sounded insulting, but… 'I didn't mean it that way.'

'Actually, I think you did. But never mind. I don't really care.' She put her earrings in, shaking her hair over her shoulders. 'Let's just get this day over with, shall we?'

Luca hesitated, wanting to defuse her anger, but sensing that she wasn't in the mood to be placated. Wordlessly he headed into the bathroom to shower.

As soon as the door closed Hannah released a shaky breath and slumped onto the divan. She couldn't take much more of this ping-ponging from one emotion to the next, from overwhelming desire to incredible rage. *What was happening to her?*

She knew the answer to that one. Luca Moretti was. She took a steadying breath, and then, taking advantage of Luca being in the shower, reached for her phone.

Diane answered on the first ring. 'Hey, Mum,' Hannah said, her voice sounding weary and just a little bit wobbly. 'It's me.'

'Hannah. Are you all right?'

'Why— Do I sound that bad?' She tried for a laugh, pressing a hand to her forehead. It didn't help her seesawing emotions that she'd got very little sleep last night.

'You sound tired,' Diane admitted cautiously. 'Is everything okay?'

'Fine. Just an intense work weekend.' Work being the word she could drop from that sentence. 'Is Jamie awake yet?'

'Yes, he's just having his breakfast. I'll put him on for you.'

Hannah closed her eyes, listening to the familiar sound of her mother's murmur, her son's excited answer. The squeak of a chair, and then the sound of him scrabbling for the phone.

'Mummy?'

A tidal wave of homesickness crashed over her, threatening to pull her under. 'Hello, sweetheart. I miss you.'

'I miss you, too. Nana says you're on an island.'

'Yes, it's very pretty. I'll try to bring you back a present. Maybe some shells or rocks for your collection?'

'Ooh, yes,' Jamie crowed. 'Can you bring back a big one? A conch?'

'I don't know about that,' Hannah said with a little laugh. 'I think they might be protected. But I'll bring you back something, Jamie, I promise. Be good for Nana now.'

'I will.'

'He always is,' Diane assured her when Hannah had said goodbye to her son. 'Don't work too hard.'

'I always work hard,' Hannah answered, and heard how grim she sounded. Maybe she did work too hard. Maybe the sacrifices weren't worth it, no matter what she believed about being financially independent and free. 'I love you, Mum,' she said.

'Hannah, are you sure you're all right…?'

'I'm fine,' Hannah said, and then, hearing the bathroom door open, she quickly said goodbye and disconnected the call.

She was just putting the phone away when Luca emerged from the bathroom, freshly shaven, his hair damp, a towel slung low on his hips. 'Were you on the phone?'

Hannah turned away from the alluring sight of his nearly naked body. 'Is that a crime?'

Luca sighed. 'No, of course not. I just wondered.'

'Then the answer is yes, I was.'

'Hannah, look, I said I was sorry.'

'In about the worst way possible.'

'Can we please call a truce?'

Hannah took a deep breath, knowing she was being childish and emotional. She was a professional, for heaven's sake, and Luca was her boss. She could handle this. 'I'm sorry,' she said evenly. 'Let's forget it. Clean slate today, all right?' She turned to him with a bright, determined smile just as Luca dropped his towel.

CHAPTER SEVEN

HANNAH WHIRLED AWAY from the sight of Luca's naked body, one hand clapped to her eyes.

She let out a trembling laugh. 'You are so not making this easier.'

'I'm sorry. I don't like dressing in the bathroom.'

'That message has been received, trust me.'

'I'm dressed now,' Luca told her dryly, and Hannah lowered her hand.

'Wearing a pair of boxer briefs does not, in my opinion, constitute dressed.'

'The important bits are covered,' he answered and reached for a shirt.

'I don't understand you,' Hannah said slowly. 'You flirt and drop your clothes and act like it's ridiculous for me to be outraged, and then you get angry with me and basically accuse me of being a slut for responding when you're practically naked next to me.' She tried for a wry smile but felt too confused and weary to manage it. 'I thought it was women who usually sent mixed messages.'

Luca stilled, his hands on the buttons of his shirt, his gaze lowered. 'This is a new situation for me,' he admitted gruffly. 'And a tense one. I know I'm acting out of character.'

'Considering you're acting as my fiancé, you certainly

are.' She sighed and reached for the strappy sandals that went with her sundress. 'So what is the schedule for today, anyway?'

'You spend the day with the other wives, touring the island, and I give my presentation.'

'Wow, that's not sexist or anything.'

Luca arched an eyebrow and resumed buttoning his shirt. 'You're not here as my PA.'

'Well I know. So you spend your day in the boardroom while I fend off Daniela's digs?'

'She's harmless. I barely know her.'

'She might disagree.' Hannah hesitated, noticing the lines of strain from Luca's nose to mouth, the fatigue she could see in his eyes and the weary set of his shoulders. She felt a surprising dart of sympathy and even compassion for him. For whatever reason, this weekend was difficult for him. 'So what is your presentation about?'

He stilled for a second and then reached for a pair of charcoal-grey trousers. 'How I'm going to rehabilitate the Tyson brand.'

'The resorts did look a bit shabby on the website.'

'They're tired,' Luca affirmed with a terse nod. 'They haven't been updated in over twenty years.'

'Why is Tyson selling them, anyway? Don't his children want to take over his business?'

A grim smile curved Luca's mouth. 'No, they're not interested.'

'That's sad, considering what a family man he is.'

'Heartbreaking,' Luca agreed dryly. He selected a cobalt-blue tie and began to knot it. There was, Hannah reflected, something quite sexy about a man putting on a tie, long, lean fingers manipulating the bright silk. Especially a man who looked like Luca.

'So what are your plans for the resorts?' she asked as she forced her gaze away from the mesmerising sight of

Luca getting dressed. 'How are you going to rehabilitate them? I never printed any documents out about it.'

'No, I did it myself.' He slid her a quick smile. 'I am capable of working a printer, despite how often I ask you to do it.'

'May I see them?' Hannah asked, and surprise flashed across Luca's face. 'I'm curious.'

His fingers slowed as he finished knotting his tie, his forehead furrowed. 'All right,' he said at last, and he went to his briefcase and took out a manila folder of documents.

Hannah joined him on the divan, their thighs nudging, while Luca opened the folder and took out the presentation he'd put together. The colourful image on the front page was an architect's visualisation of what the resort could look like, with villas in different pastel colours, cascading pools with water slides and whirlpools, and lots of colourful flowers and shrubbery. It looked inviting and fresh and friendly.

Hannah reached over to turn a page, scanning the paragraphs that described Luca's plans in detail. She knew Luca's real-estate projects always focused on sustainable energy and recyclable materials, and this was no different. But this proposal went a step further, and sought to incorporate the local culture and economy of each of the islands where there was a Tyson resort, instead of making it an exclusive enclave behind high stone walls, separate from the local residents.

She saw how family-friendly it was too, with hotel rooms and changing areas to accommodate both children and adults. Jamie would love the cascading pools and water slides outlined in one of the resorts' plans. She glanced up at Luca, who was frowning down at the images.

'For someone who doesn't have children, this is very astute.'

He shrugged one powerful shoulder. 'I did the research.'

'I like it,' she said and handed the folder back to him. 'I really like it.' Luca might have done the research, but there had been a passion and commitment to his ideas that spoke of more than just having a finger on the marketing pulse. It surprised and touched her, and it felt as if his plans for the resort had revealed something about him, something he didn't even seem to realise. He *cared.*

The last of her reservation about performing in this fake engagement fell away. She was here, and she'd agreed to help Luca. She was going to do the job properly, and maybe she'd even have fun while she was at it.

'Okay,' she said as she stood up with a bright smile. 'It's time to face the fearsome Daniela.'

A smile tugged at Luca's mouth. 'She's not that bad.'

'Why didn't it work out between you two, anyway?' Hannah asked lightly, ignoring the sting of jealousy her question caused.

'She was too clingy.'

'What, she wanted to stay the night?' Hannah quipped.

'I told you. It never got that far. Anyway, last night you agreed with me that relationships weren't worth it,' Luca reminded her.

Hannah stilled. How had they got onto this? 'I said "maybe",' she corrected him. 'The verdict is still out.'

'But you're not in a relationship?' Luca pressed, his gaze narrowed.

Hannah cocked her head. 'Is that really any of your business?'

Luca's gaze flicked to the bed, reminding him all too well of what had just happened there. 'Considering the nature of this weekend,' he answered, 'yes.'

'Fine. No, I'm not.' And hadn't been in anything close to one for over five years. 'Work keeps me busy,' she added before turning away.

They left the bedroom to join the other guests for coffee and pastries in the spacious front hall. A marble table held a huge centrepiece of lilies, and Hannah saw Luca's mouth compress as he turned away from the ostentatious display. She knew he disliked lilies, but now she wondered at the nature of that particular quirk. She was curious about Luca in a lot of new and unsettling ways, thanks to the nature of this weekend.

After about half an hour of chit-chat, Andrew Tyson called the men away to his private office for a day of presentations. Meanwhile one of his staff ushered the three women towards a waiting car, where they would be given a tour of Santa Nicola.

Hannah was looking forward to seeing some of the island, but she didn't relish Daniela's hostile company. Fortunately the third woman of their trio, Rose, plopped herself next to Hannah and chatted to her about her three young children for the drive into the island's one town, Petra. Daniela sat in the back, sulking and staring out of the window.

Hannah spent a surprisingly enjoyable morning, strolling through Petra's cobbled streets, admiring the whitewashed buildings with their colourfully painted shutters and terracotta roof tiles.

At an open-air market she bought a wooden toy boat with a sail made of shells for Jamie, smiling to think of him receiving the present. It was even better than a conch shell.

'And who is that for?' Daniela asked, coming up next to her at the stall of toys in the market square. Hannah accepted the paper-wrapped boat from the vendor with a smile of thanks. She'd managed to avoid Daniela for most of the day, but she supposed a confrontation was inevitable. Daniela dripped with the venom of a woman scorned.

'It's a boat,' she said pleasantly. 'For my nephew.' She didn't like lying about her son, but Daniela was the last person she'd trust with any confidence, and her having a child Luca didn't know about would shatter any illusions that their engagement was real.

Daniela raised perfectly plucked eyebrows. 'Have you met Luca's parents yet?' she asked, and Hannah tensed.

The question might seem innocent enough, but she knew Daniela well enough to know it was loaded. She tucked the present for Jamie in the straw bag she'd brought, stalling for time. Luca had told her to stick as close to the truth as she could, so she supposed that was what she'd have to do.

'No, I haven't,' she said as she looked into Daniela's pinched face, trying for a pleasant tone and smile. 'Not yet.'

'Not yet?' Daniela repeated, a sneer entering her voice and twisting her pretty features. 'Then you don't know he's an orphan? His parents died when he was young.' She smirked in triumph and Hannah tried to school her features into an acceptably bland expression although inwardly she cursed herself. She knew Daniela had been setting her up somehow. She'd seemed to suspect her from the start. *Because you're not the kind of woman Luca Moretti is normally seen with. Certainly not the kind of woman he'd fall in love with.*

'We had a whirlwind courtship,' she dismissed as best she could. 'We're still learning all sorts of things about each other.'

'We went on one date and he told me,' Daniela returned.

'One date?' Hannah couldn't keep from matching the woman's cattiness. 'Then perhaps it's time you got over him.'

The conversation dogged her for the rest of the day, and she breathed a sigh of relief when they headed back to the resort. Luca wasn't in the bedroom when she arrived, and she put her purchases away before running a deep bubble bath. Before dropping them off, the member of staff had informed the three women of the evening's itinerary: cocktails on the terrace with Tyson and his family, followed by a formal dinner and dancing.

Hours and hours of pretending, a prospect that made Hannah feel both tense and exhausted, even as she tingled with anticipation at spending an evening with Luca. Would he dance with her? The thought of swaying silently with him, breathing in his heat and scent, his arms strong about her, was enough to make her stomach flip-flop.

Which was *fine*, Hannah assured herself. So she was attracted to Luca. What woman wouldn't be? Why shouldn't she enjoy dancing with him? It wasn't as if it were going anywhere. She wasn't looking for a relationship or even a one-night stand. Both were too risky. All she wanted was a few moments of enjoyment and pleasure.

Except Luca had admitted he was attracted to her. Reluctantly, yes, and to his surprise, but *still*. Over the course of the day she'd got over the sting of his obvious bemusement at being attracted to her, and accepted the compliment that it was.

The door to the bedroom opened just as Hannah was stepping out of the bathroom, swathed in an enormous terrycloth bathrobe.

'How did it go?' she asked and then watched in dismay as Luca jerked his tie from his collar and strode over to the minibar, pouring himself two fingers' worth of whisky and downing it in one hard gulp.

'Fine.'

Hannah knotted the sash on her robe and pulled her damp hair out from under its thick collar. 'You're not acting like it's fine,' she observed cautiously.

'I said it was fine, it's fine,' Luca snapped, and poured another drink.

Hannah watched him, wondering what demon was riding his back. Because that was what Luca looked like: a man who was haunted. Tormented. And she didn't understand why.

'Daniela asked me about your parents,' she said, knowing she needed to tell him what had happened that afternoon. Luca stiffened, his glass halfway raised to his lips.

'Why would she do that?'

'Because she was trying to trip me up. I think she suspects something.'

'Daniela?' He shook his head, the movement curtly dismissive. 'I barely know the woman. I haven't seen her in over a year. She's been married to James Garrison for nearly six months.'

'Well, I think she still holds a candle for you. And she asked me about your parents and I told her I hadn't met them. Yet.' She waited, but Luca's face was blank.

'And?' he said after a pause.

'And she informed you were an orphan. I didn't know that, Luca, and clearly I should have. *She* knew it.'

Hannah couldn't tell anything from his expression; his eyes looked pitilessly blank. 'I'm sorry,' she said inadequately. 'For your loss.'

'It was a long time ago.'

'Still, it's a big thing.' She knew that all too well. 'And now Daniela knows I didn't know it.'

Luca pressed his lips together and tossed his empty glass on top of the bar, where it clattered and then rolled onto its side. 'There's nothing we can do about it now.'

'All right.' Hannah didn't know how to handle him in this mood; his usual energy had been transformed into a disturbing restlessness, a latent anger. 'I just thought you should know.'

'Fine. I know.'

Stung, Hannah did not reply. The tentative enjoyment she'd been nurturing for this evening was draining away like her cold bathwater. If Luca stayed in this foul mood, the night was going to be interminable.

'I'll go get ready," she said stiffly, and went to gather her clothes. She was definitely changing in the bathroom.

Luca stared at the closed bathroom door and swore under his breath. The afternoon with Tyson had been nearly unbearable, the latent fury he'd felt for so long bubbling far too close to the surface, threatening to spill over. Maintaining a professional manner had been the acting job of the century; all he'd wanted to do was haul Tyson out of his chair by his lapels and slap the smug smile off his face.

He hadn't expected to be this angry, this raw. He'd thought he'd mastered his emotions far better than that, and it only exacerbated his fury to know that he hadn't. But he shouldn't have taken it out on Hannah.

As for Daniela's suspicions… Raking a hand through his hair, Luca swore again. If his fake engagement was exposed, the humiliation he'd face in front of the man who had flayed him once already would be unendurable. He could not even contemplate it.

Luca's mouth twisted grimly as he considered the options. If Daniela or anyone suspected something, then he and Hannah would have to make doubly sure that they were convincing. Striding towards the wardrobe, he reached for his tux.

He was just straightening his bow tie when Hannah emerged from the bathroom, her chin held high, her eyes veiled. Luca's gaze dropped to her dress and his throat went dry. It was the one she'd modelled at the boutique, ice-blue with a plunging neckline only partially obscured by the gauzy overlay. She'd styled her hair in an elegant chignon, exposing the delicate, swanlike curve of her neck.

'It's all right, isn't it?' Hannah asked, nervousness making her voice wobble a bit.

'Yes…' Luca's voice came out gruff and hoarse.

Hannah tugged at the material self-consciously. 'It's just you're looking at me strangely.'

'It's only…' He cleared his throat. 'You look beautiful, Hannah.'

Colour flared in her face. 'So why are you glaring, then?' She turned away, fidgeting with her earrings, her necklace, clearly uncomfortable in the sexy, diaphanous gown.

'Hannah.' Luca crossed the room to put a hand on her shoulder, her skin cool and soft beneath his palm. 'I'm sorry I've been in such a foul mood. It's not fair to you.' He paused and then admitted with more honesty than he'd been planning to give, 'Nothing about this weekend has been fair to you.'

Hannah bowed her head, a tendril of soft brown hair falling against her cheek, making Luca want to tuck it behind her ear, trail his fingers along her skin. 'I was actually looking forward to this evening, you know,' she admitted. 'Until…'

'Until I returned to our room?' Luca finished with a wry wince, and then sighed. 'I am sorry. You don't deserve to bear the brunt of my bad mood.'

'So many apologies.' She turned around, a teasing smile curving her lips. 'I should record this conversation, otherwise I might never believe it actually happened.'

'I'll deny it, of course,' he teased back. He'd dropped his hand from her shoulder when she'd turned around but he itched to touch her again. Her waist looked so tiny he thought he could span it with his hands. The gauzy overlay of the dress made him want to peel it away and touch the pale, creamy flesh beneath. He remembered untying the halter top of the dress back when she'd first tried it on and he wanted to do it again. He wanted her…and he could tell she wanted him.

He saw it in the way she swallowed convulsively, her eyes huge and dark in her pale face. She bit her lip and Luca nearly groaned aloud. The attraction he felt for his PA was both overwhelming and inconvenient, but in that moment he couldn't even think about the consequences, the difficulties, the dangers. He just wanted to touch her.

And so he did.

He reached out with one finger and stroked her cheek; her skin was just as soft as he'd imagined, silky and cool. She shuddered under his touch, her whole body quivering in response, and that made Luca ache all the more.

'Hannah…' he began, although he didn't even know what he would say. How much he would admit.

Hannah didn't let him finish. She took a halting step away, nearly tripping on the trailing hem of her gown. 'It's—it's getting late,' she stammered. 'We should go.'

And Luca told himself he felt relieved and not crushingly disappointed that he'd had such a narrow escape.

CHAPTER EIGHT

HANNAH SIPPED THE frothy cocktail Andrew Tyson had insisted she try, an island speciality involving fruit and strong liquor, and tried to soothe the ferment inside her. Now more than ever she felt confused and disturbed, and, more alarmingly, *tempted* by Luca Moretti.

She couldn't understand how one moment he could be so aggravating and arrogant and the next so sweet and sincere. She'd gone from wanting to slug him to wanting to purr under that single, seductive stroke of his finger. The tiniest touch had created a blaze of want inside her that was still making her hot and bothered. She imagined what he could do with his whole hand, his whole body, and felt another sizzling dart of heat arrow through her.

She could not start thinking about Luca Moretti that way. All right, yes, his sex appeal had started affecting her ever since they'd left their normal employer–employee relationship behind at the office, but she hadn't taken it *seriously.* She hadn't actually entertained the possibility of something happening between them.

Now her mind skirted around that intriguing thought, flirted with the possibility of—what? A fling? A one-night stand? Hannah was sensible enough to know Luca Moretti wasn't interested in anything more, and she wasn't interested in any relationship, much less one with a man who had sworn off marriage and children, and was a notorious womaniser. But she wasn't the type to have casual sex; she never had before. And to contemplate it with her *boss*...

And yet desire was a powerful thing. The sight of him in his tuxedo was enough to make her head spin and her mouth dry. The crisp white shirt emphasised his bronzed skin, and the tuxedo jacket fit his broad shoulders and narrow hips perfectly. He was incredible, darkly magnificent, so next to him James Garrison looked like a weedy fop, Simon Tucker a corpulent would-be Santa Claus. Luca was literally head and shoulders above the other men, a gorgeous, arrogant Colossus who looked as if he could straddle the world. The only man who nearly matched his height was Andrew Tyson, and his shoulders were stooped with age, his face lined and eyes faded.

Luca had spent the first part of the evening by her side, charming and solicitous to everyone, clearly working the room. When Tyson had entered the opulent sitting room, Luca had slid an arm around Hannah's waist, practically gluing her to his side. The bump of his hip against hers was enough to make sensation sizzle through her. She could feel the heat of his thigh through the thin material of her dress, and her insides tightened to an exquisite, aching point of desire.

She'd never responded so physically, so overwhelmingly, to a man before. Not, Hannah acknowledged, that she had a lot of experience. Ben, Jamie's father, had been her only lover, and while she'd enjoyed being with him she hadn't felt this desperate, craving physical touch like water in a parched desert.

Sliding sideways glances at Luca, she felt an overwhelming urge to touch him, to feel the rough stubble on his jaw, to discover if his lips felt soft or hard against hers. To feel his body against hers as she had that morning, and rock against him again, and then deeper still.

Heat flashed through her at the thought and Luca must have felt it, must have sensed her response, because he gave her a single, burning look before turning back to address Simon Tucker.

He knew how he affected her, maybe even how much. The thought would have been mortifying except that she knew she affected him too. He'd told her he'd been attracted to her that morning, and surely she couldn't feel this kind of chemistry if it were merely one-sided.

So the question was, could she do anything about it? Did she dare? She wasn't looking for a relationship, wouldn't put herself or Jamie at risk of being hurt. She knew what happened when you loved people. You risked losing them. She'd lost too many times already to try again.

'Hannah?' Luca prompted, and she realised she had no idea what anyone had been saying for the last few minutes.

'Sorry?' She tried for a conciliatory yet loving smile. 'I'm afraid I was a million miles away.'

'No doubt planning your wedding,' Simon joked good-naturedly. 'Have you set a date?'

'As soon as possible, as far as I'm concerned,' Luca answered swiftly, with a squeeze of Hannah's waist. 'But Hannah wants more of a do.'

Hannah lifted her shoulders in a helpless shrug. 'You only get married once.'

'Hopefully,' James joked, an edge to his voice that made a frozen silence descend on the little group for a few seconds.

'What's your secret to a happy marriage, then, James?' Simon asked, trying for jocular.

'A limit-free credit card and no questions asked,' James replied with a pointed look at his wife. Daniela pressed her lips together and said nothing.

Hardly a response of a family man, Hannah thought.

James Garrison was a slick study, and looked to share Luca's view on relationships.

'I'll take that on board,' Luca answered in a tone that suggested he would do no such thing.

'Falling for your PA isn't like you, is it, Luca?' James said, malice entering his ice-blue eyes. 'I thought you made sure never to mix business and pleasure.'

'As I said last night, this time it was impossible to resist.' He glanced down at Hannah, who tilted her head up to look at him so their mouths were only a few inches apart. She felt her insides shudder even though she knew Luca was only play-acting. That simmering heat in his eyes might not have been real, but the response Hannah's body gave certainly was. Her lips parted in helpless expectation, her whole being trained on Luca's sleepy, hooded gaze.

'Irresistible,' he murmured, and then closed those scant inches separating them.

The feel of his mouth on hers was a complete surprise and yet also a sigh of relief and wonder. *At last.* Her mouth opened underneath his and Hannah clutched at his lapels, barely aware of what she was doing. Luca's tongue swept into her mouth with sure possession, turning her insides weak and liquid. Her fingers tightened on his jacket.

'No doubt that you two are heading for the altar,' Simon joked, and Luca finally broke the kiss. Hannah sagged against him, her heart thudding, her mind spinning, her whole body feeling as if she'd been lit up inside like a firework.

'Like I said,' Luca said with a wry smile. 'Irresistible. I didn't stand a chance.'

And neither did she.

Her lips were still buzzing from his kiss when they headed out to the terrace where tables had been set up for dinner, laden with crystal and silver that glinted under the moonlight. Torches flickered, casting warm shadows across the terrace, and the sea was no more than a gleam of blackness in the distance, the tide a gentle shooshing sound as the waves lapped the shore.

They were just about to take their seats when Andrew Tyson turned expectantly to the open French windows. 'Ah,' he said, his voice filled with pleasure. 'My family has finally arrived from New York. Please let me introduce you all to my wife and children.'

Luca froze before slowly turning to face the French windows, where Andrew Tyson's wife, Mirabella, and their two children stood, framed by the gauzy white curtains.

He'd been waiting for this moment, both expecting and bracing himself for it, and yet now that it was finally here he found every thought had emptied from his head, the smile wiped from his face. Even the electric, intoxicating buzz of Hannah's kiss was forgotten in that horrendous, endless moment.

Distantly, as if he were down a long tunnel, he heard people exchanging pleasantries. Words were said, but it was as if everyone had started speaking another language. Tyson's two children, Stephen and Laura, came forward, smiling and shaking hands. Stephen had the dark hair of his mother and Tyson's brown eyes. Laura was the opposite, with her father's sandy hair and her mother's blue eyes. They were both relaxed, friendly, completely in their element, and in a few seconds he was going to have to shake their hands. Say hello. Act normal.

He acknowledged this even as he didn't move. Had no idea what the expression on his face was. Felt nothing but the relentless, painful thud of his heart. He'd been waiting for this moment for years, decades, and yet he hadn't been prepared for it, not remotely.

Then he felt a soft, slender hand slide into his, fingers squeezing tightly, imbuing warmth and strength. He glanced down at Hannah's face, the worry and concern in her eyes, the compassion in her smile, and he felt as if he'd fallen out of that tunnel with a thud, as if he'd rejoined reality, and was strong enough to deal with it—thanks to the woman next to him.

'Stephen. Laura.' His voice came out on a croak that he quickly covered, extending his hand for them both to shake. 'Luca Moretti and my fiancée, Hannah Stewart.'

Hannah stepped forward to greet them both and Luca forced himself to breathe normally, to school the expression on his face into one of friendly interest. To will his heart rate to slow.

He felt the delayed reaction of shock kick in, an icy wave that swept over him and left his knees weak, his whole body near to trembling. He had to get out of there.

'If you'll excuse me,' he murmured, and went in search of the bathroom.

Once inside, safely away from all the prying eyes, he splashed his face with cold water and then stared hard into the mirror, willing himself to get a grip. He'd climbed his way out of appalling poverty, negotiated dozens of million-and billion-dollar deals, was a man of power and authority and wealth. He'd conquered all these old fears and insecurities. He didn't need to feel this way now. He *wouldn't*.

Except he did.

He released a shuddering breath and rubbed a hand over his face. He needed to get back to the dinner. James Garrison was chomping at the bit to take this deal out from under him, simply out of spite. Garrison had always been jealous of Luca's success, of the huge deals he brokered that James hadn't a chance in hell of managing. Luca knew he couldn't afford to throw himself a damned pity party in the bathroom.

Taking a deep breath, he straightened his tux and then

opened the door to the hall, stopping short when he saw Hannah there waiting for him.

'What are you—?'

'I was worried about you.' She put a hand on his sleeve, and he glanced down at her fingers, long and slender, the nails buffed and glistening with clear varnish. Every part of her was simple and yet so elegant. 'Luca, what's going on? Can't you tell me?'

'It's nothing.'

'That's not true.' Concern threaded her voice. 'Please, Luca. Do you know how hard it is to act the part when I have no idea what you're going through?'

'You're doing fine, Hannah.' He shrugged off her hand. 'You certainly acted the part when I kissed you.'

Colour surged into her face but her gaze was steady, her voice calm. 'Don't take out your frustrations on me, Luca. All I'm asking for is the truth.'

He raked a hand through his hair, knowing she had a right to understand at least a little of what was going on. 'Tyson and I have a history,' he said in a low voice. 'Not a pleasant one. I didn't expect it, but seeing him again brings it all back.'

'And his family?' Hannah asked. Luca tensed.

'What about his family?'

'You obviously didn't like their arrival. You went white—'

'I did not,' he denied shortly, even though it was pointless. Hannah was gazing at him in a cringing mixture of pity and disbelief.

'Luca—'

'We need to get back in there.' He cut her off, and then reached for her hand. Tonight he'd show Andrew Tyson and his damned family just how much he had, how happy he was.

By the time they arrived back on the terrace, everyone

was seated and the first course had been served. Luca and Hannah took their places with murmured apologies. Luca saw he was seated next to Stephen Tyson, and he braced himself to talk to the man.

Stephen, he knew, had chosen not to take on the family's business but was a doctor in New York instead. Now he gave Luca a friendly smile.

'I'm sorry, but have we met before?'

A hollow laugh echoed through the emptiness inside him and he swallowed it down. 'No, I'm quite sure we haven't.'

Luca could feel Hannah's concern, the tension tautening her slender body. It was strange how attuned they'd become to each other and their moods, but perhaps that was simply an effect of the parts they had to play.

'Really?' Stephen shrugged, still smiling. 'Strange, but you look familiar.'

'Perhaps you've seen his photograph in one of the industry magazines?' Hannah suggested with a smile of her own. 'Luca is quite famous in his own right.' She placed a hand over his, squeezing his fingers, and Luca felt his heart twist inside him. He'd never had someone fight his corner before, even in the smallest way. He'd always been alone, had gone through childhood with his fists up and his nose bloody. Seeing Tyson made him feel like that battered boy again, and yet having Hannah hold his hand reminded him that he wasn't.

'Of course you are,' Stephen acknowledged. 'I know you developed the cancer centre in Ohio. It was really a masterwork of art and functionality. Utterly brilliant.'

'Thank you,' Luca said gruffly. He hadn't expected Stephen Tyson to be so friendly and sincere. It made it hard to hate him.

Somehow he managed to get through three courses, making small talk, smiling when necessary. He'd brought

Hannah's hand underneath the table after the first course to rest on his thigh and he wrapped his fingers around hers, clinging to her, craving her warmth. She didn't let go.

As the coffee and petits fours were being served, Andrew Tyson rose to make a toast.

'It's such a pleasure to have three dedicated family men here,' he began with a genial smile for all of them. 'As someone who has always determined to put family first, it is of course important to me that the man who takes on Tyson Resorts share my values.' He paused, his smiling gaze moving to his wife and then to his children. 'While I am saddened that my own children have not chosen this task, I understand completely why they've decided to pursue their own dreams—as I of course wish them to. My children are my pride and my joy, the touchstone of my life, along with my wife. The happiness I've experienced with my family is what I wish for each of you, and for every family who visits a Tyson resort.'

Luca couldn't bear to hear any more. He shifted in his seat, and Hannah squeezed his hand in warning. He couldn't leave now, but he could at least tune out Tyson's words.

Finally Tyson raised his glass and everyone else did as well, murmuring 'Hear, hear...' dutifully. Luca drained his glass of wine and then pulled away from Hannah.

'Luca,' she began, but he just shook his head.

'Later,' he managed, and then strode down the terrace steps, out into the darkness.

Hannah dabbed her mouth with her napkin, trying to cover the worry that she was sure was visible on her face. What kind of terrible history could Luca possibly have with Andrew Tyson? She glanced at the man who was now chatting with Simon and Rose Tucker, and decided she would make her excuses as well. If Luca left without her, it might look as if they were having a lovers' tiff. If they both left, people might assume it was a romantic tryst instead.

She made her farewells to the Tysons, telling them that Luca had wanted to steal her away for a moonlit walk on the beach.

'Ah, young love,' Andrew answered with a genial smile. 'There's nothing like it.'

No indeed, Hannah thought grimly as she held handfuls of her dress to keep from tripping down the stone steps that led directly to the beach.

Away from the candlelit terrace, the beach was awash in darkness, the white sand lit only by a pale sickle of moon. Hannah couldn't see Luca anywhere. Impatiently she kicked off the silver stiletto heels that made walking in sand impossible, and gathered a big handful of gauzy dress around her knees so she could walk unimpeded. Then she set off in search of her erstwhile fiancé.

CHAPTER NINE

HANNAH FOUND LUCA about half a mile down the beach, away from the villa, with nothing but a few palm trees for company. He sat with his elbows resting on his knees, his head cradled in his hands. Hannah had never seen such an abject pose; every powerful line of Luca's body seemed to radiate despair.

She hesitated, not wanting to intrude on his moment of sorrowful solitude, but not wanting to leave him alone either. He looked too lonely.

'I'm not going to bite your head off,' Luca said, his voice low and so very weary. 'Although you have good reason to think I would.'

She came closer, her dress trailing on the sand that was cool and silky under her bare feet.

'I wasn't thinking that,' she said quietly, and came to sit beside him, drawing her knees up as his were. He didn't lift his head. She thought about asking him yet again what pain and secrets he was hiding, but she didn't think there was much point. Luca didn't want to tell her and, truthfully, she didn't blame him. She had pain and secrets of her own she didn't want spilling out. Still, she felt she had to say something.

'The petits fours weren't actually that good,' she ventured after a moment. 'So you really didn't miss much.'

Luca let out a soft huff of laughter, and somehow that sounded sad too.

'I know what it's like to grieve, Luca,' Hannah said quietly.

'Is that what you think I'm doing?'

'I don't know, and I won't ask because I know you don't want to tell me. But...' she let out her breath slowly '...I know what it's like to feel angry and cheated and in despair.'

'Do you?' Luca lifted his head to gaze at her speculatively; she could only just make out the strong lines and angles of his face in the moonlit darkness. 'Who do you grieve, Hannah?'

It was such a personal question, and one whose answer she didn't talk about much. Yet she was the one who had started this conversation, and if Luca wasn't able to talk about his pain, perhaps she should talk about hers.

'My father, for one,' Hannah answered. 'He died when I was fifteen.'

'I'm sorry.' Luca stared straight ahead, his arms braced against his knees. 'How did it happen?'

'A heart attack out of the blue. He went to work and dropped dead at his desk. It was a complete shock to everyone.'

'Which must have made it even harder.'

'Yes, in a way. My mother wasn't prepared emotionally, obviously, or financially.'

Luca glanced at her. 'Your father didn't leave her provided for?'

'No, not really. He'd always meant to take out a life insurance policy, but he never got around to it. He was only forty-two years old. And savings were slim... He wasn't irresponsible,' she hastened to add. 'Just not planning for the disaster that happened.' And she'd decided long ago not to be bitter about that. She'd simply chosen to make different choices.

'So what did your mother do?'

'Got a job. She'd been a housewife for sixteen years, since before I was born, and she'd been a part-time preschool teacher before that. It was tough to find work that earned more than a pittance.'

'And what about you?'

'I worked too, after school. We sold our house and rented a small flat. That helped with expenses.' But it had been hard, so hard, to go from the simple, smiling suburban life she'd had as a child to working all hours and living in a small, shabby flat.

'I'm sorry,' Luca said again. 'I never knew.'

'I never told you.' She paused, waiting for him to volunteer something of his own situation, but he didn't. 'What about you?' she asked at last. 'What happened to your parents?'

Luca was silent for a long moment. 'My mother died when I was fourteen.'

'I'm sorry.'

His cynical smile gleamed in the darkness. 'We're both so sorry, aren't we? But it doesn't change anything.'

'No, but sometimes it can make you feel less alone.'

'How do you know I feel alone?'

She took a deep breath. 'Because I do, sometimes.' Another breath. 'Do you?'

Luca didn't answer for a long moment. 'Yes,' he said finally. 'Yes, all the time.' He let out a hollow laugh. 'And no more so than when I was looking at Andrew Tyson and his damn kids.' His voice broke on the words and he averted his head from her, hiding his face, shielding his emotion.

'Oh, Luca.' Hannah's voice broke too, for her heart ached to see this proud, powerful man brought to such sadness.

'Don't.' His voice was muffled, his head still turned away from her. 'Don't pity me, Hannah. I couldn't bear it.'

'I don't—'

'I'd rather someone attacked me than pitied me. It's the worst kind of violence, cloaked as something kind or virtuous.' He spoke scathingly, the words spat out, making her wonder.

'Who pitied you, Luca?' she asked quietly. 'Because you seem the least likely person for anyone ever to feel sorry for.'

'I wasn't always.'

'When you were a child? When you lost your mother?'

He nodded tersely. 'Yes. Then.'

But she felt he wasn't telling her the whole truth. 'What happened to you after your mother's death? Did you live with your father?'

'No, he wasn't around.' Luca expelled a low breath. 'I went into foster care, and managed to secure a scholarship to a boarding school in Rome. It saved me, lifted me up from the gutter, but not everyone liked that fact. I stayed on my own.'

It sounded like a terribly lonely childhood. Even though she'd lost her father, Hannah was grateful for the fifteen years of happy memories that he'd given her. 'How did your mother die?' she asked.

He let out a long, weary sigh and tilted his head towards the sky. 'She killed herself.'

Startled, Hannah stared at him in horror. 'Oh, but that's terrible—'

'Yes, but I could understand why she did it. Life had become unendurable.'

'But you were only fourteen—'

'I think,' Luca said slowly, still staring at the starlit sky, 'when you feel that trapped and desperate and sad, you stop thinking about anything else. You can't reason your way out of it. You can only try to end the sadness.'

Tears stung Hannah's eyes at the thought. 'You have great compassion and understanding, to be able to think that.'

'I've never been angry with her,' Luca answered flatly. He lowered his head to gaze out at the sea, washed in darkness. 'She was a victim.'

'And were you a victim?' Hannah asked. She felt as if she were feeling her way through the dark, groping with her words, trying to shape an understanding out of his reluctant half-answers.

'No, I've never wanted to think of myself as victim. That ends only in defeat.'

'I suppose I felt the same,' Hannah offered cautiously. 'My father's death left my mother in a difficult situation, and I wanted to make sure I never ended up that way as an adult.'

He gave her a swift, searching glance. 'Is that why you agreed with me that relationships aren't worth it?'

'I only said maybe,' Hannah reminded him. 'But yes, that has something to do with it.' She thought of Jamie's father and felt a lump form in her throat. She'd moved on from her grief years ago, but opening those old wounds still hurt, still made her wonder and regret. If she'd done something differently…if she'd handled their last argument better… 'When you lose someone,' she said, 'you don't feel like taking the chance again.'

'But he was your father, not a boyfriend or husband.'

'I lost one of those too,' Hannah admitted. 'A boyfriend, not a husband.' They'd never got that far. They'd never had the chance. And she had to believe that they would have, if Ben hadn't died. That he would have changed his mind, she would have had a second chance.

'When?'

'Almost six years ago.'

Luca turned to her, the moonlight washing half his face in lambent silver. 'You bear your sorrows so well. You don't look like someone haunted by grief.'

'I'm not,' Hannah answered staunchly. 'I choose not to be.' Even if it was hard, a choice she had to make every day not to wallow in grief and regret.

'That's a strong choice to make.'

'It hasn't always been easy,' Hannah allowed. 'And I can't say I haven't had my moments of self-pity or evenings alone with a tub of mint-chocolate-chip ice cream,' she added. 'But I try not to wallow.'

His mouth twisted wryly. 'Is that what you think I'm doing? Wallowing?'

Horrified, Hannah clapped a hand to her mouth. 'Luca, no—'

'No, it is.' He cut her off. 'And I despise myself for it. I thought I could come here and stare Andrew Tyson in the face. I thought I could smile and shake the man's hand and feel nothing, because I'd schooled myself to feel nothing for so long. But I can't. I *can't*.' His voice broke on a ragged gasp and he dropped his head in his hands. 'I don't want to feel this,' he muttered. 'I don't want to be enslaved by something that happened so long ago. I wanted this to be a clean slate, a second chance—' He drew in a ragged breath, his head in his hands, and Hannah did the only thing she could, the only thing she felt she could do in that moment. She hugged him.

She wrapped her arms around him, pressing her cheek into his back, trying to imbue him with her comfort. 'Oh, Luca,' she whispered. *'Luca.'*

He went rigid underneath her touch but she hung on anyway. Luca could be as strong and stoic as he liked, but he still needed comfort, and in that moment she was determined to give it to him.

He reached up to grip her wrists that were locked across his chest as if he'd force her away from him, but he didn't.

'Why are you so kind?' he demanded in a raw mutter.

'Why are you so afraid of kindness?' Hannah returned softly.

He turned, his hands still on her wrists, and for a second she thought he would reject her offer of comfort and push her away, but then his features twisted and with a muttered curse he reached for her instead.

Their mouths met and clashed and the fierce desire to comfort him turned into something far more primal and urgent. His hands were everywhere, clenching in her hair, stroking her back, cupping her breasts, and all the while his mouth didn't leave hers.

They fell back on the sand in a tangle of limbs, and when Luca's thumb brushed over the taut peak of her nipple Hannah arched into his hand, craving an even deeper caress.

She tore at his shirt, studs popping, desperate to feel his bare, glorious skin. She let out a gasp of pleasure and satisfaction when she finally parted the shirt and ran her palms along his hair-roughened chest, revelling in the feel of sculpted muscle and hot skin.

Luca's breath came out in a hiss and then he was pulling at her dress, the gauzy folds tearing under his urgent touch, and Hannah didn't even care.

'Luca,' she gasped, and it was both a demand and a plea. She needed to feel his hands on her body. She felt as if she'd explode if she didn't. He pulled the tattered dress down to her waist, leaving her completely bare on top as she hadn't worn a bra with the halter-style dress.

Then he bent his head to her breasts, his tongue now touching where his hands had been, and Hannah clutched his head to her, nearly sobbing in pleasure at the feel of him tasting her.

But even that wasn't enough. She needed more from him, of him, and when his hand slipped under her bunched dress, his fingers deftly finding and stroking her centre, she thought she almost had it. The pleasure was so acute it was akin to pain, a sharp ache that left her gasping. She skimmed the length of his erection, sucking her breath in at the way his body throbbed in insistent response to her touch. She pulled at his trousers, fumbling with the ties of his cummerbund, and with a muttered oath Luca ripped it away from him and tossed it on the sand. Hannah let out a gurgle of laughter that he swallowed with his mouth as he kissed her again and she gave herself to him, offering everything as her hands clutched at his shoulders and her hips rocked against his.

'Hannah,' Luca muttered against her mouth. 'Hannah, I need…'

'Yes,' she answered almost frantically. 'Yes, *please*, Luca, now.'

She parted her legs as he fumbled with the zip on his trousers. She didn't have a second to consider if this was a good idea, if she'd regret this afterwards. She couldn't think past the haze of overwhelming need that consumed her.

Then Luca was inside her, an invasion so sudden, so sweet, so *much*, that Hannah felt tears sting her eyes. It had been so long since she'd given her body to a man. So long since she'd felt completed, conquered. She wrapped her legs around him, enfolding herself around him as she accepted him into her body.

He stilled inside her as they both adjusted to the intense sensation. Luca's eyes were closed, his arms braced by her shoulders. Then Hannah flexed around him and with a groan of surrender he started to move.

It had been a while, and it took her a few exquisite thrusts before she managed to find the rhythm and match it, and then with each thrust she felt her body respond, opening up like a flower, everything in her spiralling upward, straining towards that glittering summit that was just out of her reach—

Until she found it, her body convulsing around Luca's as she cried out his name and the climax rushed over them both, their bodies shuddering in tandem, tears slipping down her face as she gave herself to the tidal wave of pleasure.

In the aftermath Hannah lay there, Luca's body on top of hers, the thud of his heart matching her own. She felt dazed and dizzy and yet utterly sated. She couldn't regret what had happened, not even for a second.

Then Luca rolled off her with a curse, lying on the sand on his back, one arm thrown over his eyes. Okay, maybe she could.

Hannah felt a whole bunch of things at once: the cold sand underneath her, the stickiness on her thighs, the grit in her hair, the torn dress about her waist. The pleasure that had overwhelmed her only moments before now felt like mere vapour, a ghost of a memory.

She pulled her torn dress down over herself, wincing at the shredded gauze. To think Luca had spent nine thousand pounds on this one gown. Not that she would have had a chance to wear it again, even if it hadn't been ruined.

Luca lifted his arm from his face and turned his head to rake her with one quick glance. Even in the moonlit darkness Hannah could see how indifferent he looked, and inwardly she quelled.

This had been a mistake. A wonderful, terrible mistake, and one she would most certainly regret no matter the pleasure she'd experienced. How could she work with Luca from now on? What if he fired her? But even worse than the fears for her job was the piercing loneliness of the thought that he might shut her out of his life. He already was, and she'd barely been in it to begin with.

She took a deep, calming breath and told herself not to jump to conclusions.

'Your dress,' Luca stated flatly.

Hannah glanced down at it. 'I'm afraid it's past repair.'

'I'm thinking of getting back to the room,' he clarified impatiently. 'I don't care about the dress.'

'Oh. Okay.' She bit her lip, trying not to feel hurt. This was a far cry from pillow talk, but then they hadn't even had a bed. They'd had a few moments of frenzied, mindless passion that Luca undoubtedly regretted, just as she was starting to.

Luca sat up, readjusting his trousers and then searching for the studs on his shirt. He found enough to keep the shirt mostly fastened, and he stuffed his tie and cummerbund in his pocket. Then he shrugged off his tuxedo jacket and draped it over her shoulders.

'There. You're mostly decent. Hopefully we can sneak into the room without anyone seeing us.'

'And if they do?' Hannah asked, thankful her voice didn't wobble. 'Wouldn't they just think we'd done exactly what they'd expect us to do, and made love under the stars?'

Luca's mouth compressed and he stood up, brushing the sand from his legs before he reached a hand down to her. She took it only because she knew she'd struggle getting up on her own. She was torn between an irrational anger—how had she expected Luca to act?—and a deep and disturbing hurt. She shouldn't care this much. She hadn't had *feelings* for Luca, not really.

Except somehow, in the last twenty-four hours, she had begun to develop them. She'd seen intriguing glimpses into a man whom she'd already respected and admired—glimpses of strength and emotion. She'd seen him determined and arrogant but also humble, concerned for her even while he was in the throes of his own emotional agony. Luca Moretti had depths she'd discovered this weekend that he hadn't even hinted at before.

And he was hiding them all from her now. He dropped her hand the moment she was upright and started walking back towards the villa, its lights glimmering in the distance. Hannah followed him, clutching his jacket around her shoulders, wincing at the sand she could feel in her hair and clothes.

They skirted around the terrace that was now empty to the other side of the house, where the bedrooms' French windows overlooked the beach.

'You'd better pick the right room,' Hannah muttered darkly. Hurt and anger were giving way to a weary resignation as she scrambled to think of a way to navigate this awful aftermath.

Luca didn't even reply, just stalked ahead and then flung open a pair of windows and ushered her into their bedroom. Hannah stepped inside, her glance taking in the turned-down bed, the chocolate hearts on the pillows. Had it been only twenty-four hours ago that she'd been in this same room, this same position, except now everything felt drastically different?

'Why don't you get cleaned up?' Luca said, nodding towards the bathroom without looking at her. 'And then we'll talk.'

CHAPTER TEN

LUCA SHRUGGED OFF his torn shirt as Hannah disappeared into the bathroom. What had he been *thinking*, slaking his lust with his PA? The trouble was, he hadn't been thinking. He'd been utterly in the grip of his own awful emotions, and Hannah's tentative comfort had been the balm he'd so desperately craved. It was only afterwards, after the most sexually and emotionally explosive encounter he'd ever experienced, that the regrets came rushing in. Regret to have slept with his PA at all, and, worse, shame that he'd allowed her to see him in such a vulnerable state. What must Hannah think of him? It had practically been a pity lay.

Except she had been just as gripped by the raw, urgent need that he'd felt consume him. She'd been just as desperate to have him inside her as he'd been to be there.

The knowledge didn't make him feel any better. The whole thing was an appalling mistake, made about a thousand times worse by the fact that they hadn't used any protection.

Hannah emerged from the bathroom, dressed in the same awful pyjamas she'd worn last night, but at least tonight Luca was grateful for the way they hid her body. The last thing he needed was to feel tempted again.

She didn't look at him as she came into the room, going

directly to the bed. Her body was stiff with affront and Luca watched in bemused disbelief as she reached for her book by the bedside table and then buried her nose in it.

He took a deep breath. 'Hannah.' She didn't so much as look up from her book. 'We need to talk.'

'Oh, *now* we need to talk?' Finally she looked up, and Luca saw anger firing her brown eyes, turning them to gold. Her hair was tousled about her shoulders, her face flushed, and, pyjamas aside, she looked utterly lovely.

But he had to stop thinking that way.

'Yes, now we need to talk.'

'Not right after?' Hannah filled in. 'No, you couldn't bother to say boo to me then.'

Luca's insides tightened with both irritation and remorse. He hadn't treated her very well, back on the beach, but she'd blindsided him, in so many ways. 'Clearly what happened took us both by surprise.' She took a deep breath and nodded, her hands folded across her abandoned book. 'So much so that I didn't think to use any protection.'

Hannah's lips parted on a soundless gasp as her eyes widened in shocked realisation. 'I didn't even think of that.' She nibbled her lip. 'But it's not…I mean, based on the time of the month, I don't think it's risky.'

'You'd let me know? I mean, if…?'

Her gaze locked with his and her breath came out in a rush. Luca felt the import of the moment, the enormous impact of what they'd shared together. More than he'd ever shared with any other woman, pregnancy or not. 'Yes, of course,' she answered. '*If.* But I really don't think there's going to be an if. So that's one less thing to worry about.' She tried for a smile but it wobbled and slid off her face, and she looked away, blinking rapidly.

'Hannah…' He expelled a shaky breath. He was finding this all a lot harder than he would have wished. He didn't like the realisation that he'd hurt her.

Hannah glanced down at her laced fingers. 'You don't need to worry about me, Luca,' she said quietly. 'I wasn't looking for some kind of fairy tale, and I certainly don't have any expectations because of...well, you know.'

And that proclamation, which should have only brought blessed relief, caused him the most absurd flicker of disappointment. His emotions were clearly all over the place. 'Good,' Luca said shortly. 'Then we can forget this ever happened and move on.'

With effort Hannah kept her face blank. *Forget this ever happened.* As if she could ever do that. Those passionate moments with Luca were emblazoned on her brain, his touch branded on her body. She swallowed and nodded.

'Yes,' she agreed, because what else could she say? Luca wasn't looking for a relationship, and neither was she—and certainly not with a man like him. If she ever dared to risk her heart—and her son's—it would be with someone who valued family, who wanted a child. *Her* child.

And yet Luca had put so much care into his plans for the family resort, and just a moment ago he'd almost looked disappointed that she was most likely not pregnant.

But she couldn't go chasing after rainbows where none existed. He'd made his intentions more than clear.

Luca nodded, seemingly satisfied with her agreement. 'You'll tell me if the situation changes?'

'If I'm pregnant?' she clarified wryly. 'Yes, Luca, I'll tell you. It's not as if it's something I could hide, working for you.'

'But you wouldn't try to hide it?'

'No, of course not.' She frowned at him. 'But let's cross that bridge when we come to it, shall we?'

A terse nod was all the response she got and he disappeared into the bathroom while she tossed her book on the bedside table, too unsettled to read.

Even though she'd just told Luca they didn't need to think about how to handle a pregnancy yet, she found herself doing just that—and her scattered thoughts soon morphed into the most absurd fantasy of Luca as a doting dad. This child could have what Jamie had missed out on. She pictured Luca cradling their newborn, his big, strong hands so tender with that tiny scrap of humanity. She thought of all the things that Jamie would experience without a dad—a lost tooth, riding a bike, Christmas and birthdays. This child wouldn't miss out at all.

Then Luca came out of the bathroom and got into bed, his movements brisk and businesslike, and Hannah forced her wayward thoughts to a screeching halt. What on earth was she thinking, casting Luca Moretti of all people, into the role of a devoted father? He was anything but—not to the imaginary child they most likely hadn't conceived, and certainly not to her son by another man. If she was pregnant, he'd probably pay her off and remain completely uninvolved. The antithesis of a happily-ever-after.

No, she had to clamp down on that kind of dangerous and foolish thinking right now. Luca wasn't interested in relationships, and neither was she. As he'd told her, it simply wasn't worth it.

The next morning Hannah woke to an empty bed; she'd been so exhausted from everything that had happened, she'd fallen asleep without any restless wondering of what Luca was thinking or feeling next to her.

Now, in the bright light of a Mediterranean morning, the events of last night took on a sordid and reproachable cast. What had seemed irresistible and exciting in the sultry darkness now felt shameful. She was glad Luca wasn't in the room because she didn't think she could look him in the eye. Just the memory of how she'd begged him to touch her made Hannah's face flame.

Half an hour later, after eating breakfast delivered by staff and dressed in another one of her ensembles from Diavola, her hair and make-up done, Hannah felt more in control of the situation, or at least as if a mask of calm respectability had been put in place.

Luca hadn't returned to the room and so she decided to go in search of him. She saw several suitcases in the foyer and realised Andrew Tyson's guests were starting to depart. She'd known she and Luca would be leaving some time today, and the thought of returning home to Jamie, to her mother, to normal life, brought a rush of relief. She couldn't handle any more of her seesawing emotions.

She wandered through a few more rooms before she found some of Tyson's guests along with his family in a breakfast room, enjoying coffee and pastries. Laura Tyson gave her a friendly smile as she came into the room.

'You're Luca Moretti's fiancée, isn't that right?'

'Yes…'

'I saw the two of you sneak out at the end of the dinner last night,' Laura said confidentially, her eyes sparkling. 'I don't blame you. Luca is certainly a handsome man, and he obviously adores you.'

That sincerely delivered statement nearly made Hannah choke. 'Thank you,' she murmured. She couldn't manage any more. This awful pretence was straining at its seams. Another lie and it would explode. *She* would.

Laura leaned closer to Hannah and lowered her voice. 'To tell you the truth, I think my father favours your fiancé to take over the resorts. He mentioned how impressed he was with his plans.'

'Oh…well, that's encouraging to hear.' Hannah smiled, genuinely glad for Luca even amidst the turmoil of all her feelings. Based on the proposal she'd seen, he deserved to win the commission.

'He'll make the announcement shortly, I'm sure.'

'Today…?'

Laura wrinkled her nose. 'Probably not for a week or two. This is a big decision for him.' Her smile fell as she admitted, 'I think he's still hoping one of us will show an interest, but Stephen and I had different dreams.'

'He's a doctor…'

'And I work in pharmaceutical research. Our little sister died of leukaemia when she was only four years old,' Laura explained quietly. 'It had a big impact on all of us… and I think we've chosen to honour her memory in different ways.'

'I'm sorry for your loss,' Hannah said, knowing the words were inadequate yet meaning them utterly. She knew what it was like to lose someone at a young age.

'I'm glad that someone is interested in taking the resorts on,' Laura said. 'I know they're a bit worn. Dad hasn't had as much energy as he used to, and he's never been good at delegating. But I hope with your Luca on board things will change for the better.'

Her Luca. As if. 'I hope so too,' Hannah said and Laura gave her one more smile before turning away.

Luca came in the room a short while later, his face and body both tense. Even grim-faced as he was he looked devastatingly attractive in a grey pinstriped suit matched with a crisp white shirt and dark blue tie. The elegantly cut suit showed off his muscular body to perfection, and he strode into the room as if he owned it, his gaze searching out Hannah.

As his deep brown eyes locked with hers Hannah felt a fiery heat start a blaze in her belly, much to her irritation. She'd worked for the man for three years and he'd never caused that reaction in her in all that time. Yet right now she couldn't deny the magnetic pull of attraction that had her unable to break away from his penetrating stare. She could only pretend it didn't exist.

'Hannah.' He nodded towards the door. 'Are you ready to leave?'

No lovey-dovey play-acting this morning, she noted. He must have known that he'd sealed the deal.

'I didn't realise we were leaving so soon,' Hannah answered. 'I'll pack right away.'

Luca followed her down the hall and into their bedroom. The huge, airy room felt claustrophobic as she got out her suitcase and started neatly folding her clothes into it. Her hands trembled and she hid them in the folds of a dress.

'I spoke to Laura just now,' she said, her voice an octave higher than normal. She cleared her throat and tried again. 'She seems quite sure that you've secured the bid.'

'Tyson is keeping us on leading strings,' Luca answered. He prowled around the room, his hands shoved into his pockets, every stride predatory and restless.

'Laura said it was a big decision for him to make.'

'I think he just likes toying with us,' Luca answered dismissively. 'That's the kind of man he is.'

'If there really is bad blood between you,' Hannah said slowly, amazed that she hadn't thought of this earlier, 'why would he sell the resorts to you?'

Luca stilled, his back to her as he gazed out at the sparkling sea. 'Because he doesn't know it was me.'

'What do you mean?'

'It's complicated,' he answered on a shrug, his voice gruff. 'Suffice it to say, Tyson doesn't realise there is any history between us. Only I do.'

Hannah frowned, Luca's admission making her uneasy. How was what he'd said even possible? And yet Luca clearly meant it. He also very clearly wasn't going to tell her anything else, and she didn't want to ask. She'd got in too deep with Luca Moretti already.

'I just need to get my wash bag from the bathroom,' she said. 'And then I'll be ready to go.'

Fifteen minutes later they'd made their farewells and were bumping down the road to the airport in the same Jeep they'd arrived in only forty-eight hours ago, which seemed unbelievable. Hannah felt as if she'd lived an entire lifetime in the space of a few short and incredible days. And that lifetime, she reminded herself, was over.

An hour later they were settled in first class in the aeroplane to London. Luca waved away the offers of champagne and Hannah looked out of the window, stupidly stung. A few days ago he'd said he'd enjoyed watching her taste champagne. But she'd had quite a bit of champagne since then, and she had a feeling it would taste flat now anyway. So much for tickly.

As soon as they'd taken off Luca got some papers out of his briefcase and spent the entire flight immersed in work. Hannah told herself she was grateful not to have to make awkward small talk, but silence gave her the unwelcome space to remember every second of last night's encounter.

Just thinking about the way Luca had kissed her, with such overwhelming intensity and passion and *desperation*, made her inner muscles clench and she shifted restlessly in her seat. She *had* to get over this. Her job and her sanity were both at stake. She couldn't work with Luca every day and remember how he'd felt. How he'd tasted.

And she'd forget in time, Hannah assured herself. Of course she was still thinking about his kiss. It hadn't even been twenty-four hours. But the memory would fade in time, and who knew? Maybe in a week or month or ten years, she and Luca would laugh about the one bizarre interlude they'd had on a Mediterranean island.

Hannah settled back into her seat and started to flick through the films available on her entertainment console. Yes. That was exactly how it was going to be.

CHAPTER ELEVEN

THE NEXT MORNING Hannah dressed for work in her smartest pencil skirt and silk blouse, slipped on her highest, sharpest stiletto heels. She needed armour.

On the Tube on the way into the Moretti Enterprises office, she worried if she was making too much effort. Maybe Luca would think she was trying to impress him. But she'd nip that prospect right in the bud the second she arrived. She'd make it quite clear to Luca that she was as interested and invested as he was in getting their relationship back on a firm, professional footing.

She needed to get her life back to normal, both for Jamie's sake as well as her own. She'd had a happy reunion with her son last night, reading stories and cuddling before bed.

Once Jamie had been tucked in bed, Diane had regaled Hannah with stories of their weekend together: a trip to the zoo, baking fairy cakes on a rainy afternoon. Then her mother had cocked her head and swept her with a knowing yet inquisitive gaze.

'I didn't realise Luca Moretti was so handsome.'

'Haven't you seen his picture in the tabloids?' Hannah had answered a touch too sharply. 'He's often photographed with some socialite or other.'

'You know I don't read the tabloids.' Her mother had

sat back, arms folded. 'But going on a business trip with him was a departure from the way things usually are, wasn't it?'

That, Hannah had reflected sourly, was a complete understatement. 'Yes, it was,' she'd answered.

'Do you think you'll go on another trip with him?'

'No,' Hannah had answered firmly, and thankfully her mother hadn't asked her any more questions.

That morning as dawn light had filtered through the curtains Jamie had crept into her bedroom, teddy bear dangling from one chubby fist, and climbed into bed with her. Hannah had snuggled his warm little body against her, savouring the precious moment. It had reminded her of her priorities, and put the events of the weekend firmly into their place—a moment out of reality, nothing more.

Luca had not yet arrived when she reached the penthouse office, and Hannah breathed a sigh of relief that she had a few moments to compose herself and begin work without worrying about her boss.

She was well into her in-tray when he arrived, striding through the lift doors, looking devastatingly sexy in a navy blue suit, his close-cropped dark hair bristly and damp from the rain.

Hannah looked up as he entered, and the breath bottled in her lungs, every thought emptying from her head as her gaze locked on his body and her mind played a reel of X-rated memories. With effort she yanked her gaze away, staring down at the spreadsheet she'd been working on, the numbers blurring before her distracted gaze.

'Good morning.' Luca's voice was brisk and businesslike, giving nothing away. 'I'll be in my office if you need anything.' And he strode past her desk, closing the door behind him with a decisive click.

Hannah ignored the pinpricks of hurt and disappointment she felt at his obvious dismissal and refocused on her work.

Luca didn't emerge from his office all morning, and Hannah managed to plough through paperwork until just before lunch, when she needed Luca's signature on some letters.

She approached his door with trepidation, bracing herself for his hostility.

'Come in,' Luca barked after she knocked on the door, and she pushed it open, the letters in her hand.

'I just need you to sign these,' she murmured, and Luca beckoned her forward. It was no more than he would have done a week ago, but now the command seemed autocratic and unfeeling. Her problem, she told herself. She had to get over her unreasonable reaction to this man.

She placed the letters on the desk, taking a careful step away as he signed them so she wouldn't breathe in his cedarwood scent or feel the heat emanating from his powerful body.

'Here.' Luca handed her the letters, and his hand brushed hers as she took them. Hannah felt as if she'd been scorched. A tremor went through her body, followed by a wave of helpless longing that she knew she couldn't disguise. Everything in her yearned to have him touch her again, and this time with intent.

Luca cursed under his breath and heat surged into Hannah's face. 'I'm… I'm sorry,' she muttered, embarrassed beyond belief that her reaction was so cringingly obvious to him. 'I thought I'd go to lunch if you don't need me.' *Wrong* choice of words. 'I mean, if there's nothing you need me to do…in the office…' Could she make this any worse?

'I know what you meant,' Luca answered tersely. 'Yes, you can go.'

With relief Hannah fled from the room.

* * *

Luca watched Hannah leave his office as if she had the fires of hell on her heels, and let out a weary groan. This was all much more difficult than he'd thought it would be. Much more tempting. The merest brush of Hannah's hand against his own had made his body pulse with desire, hardly the distraction he needed during the working day.

They'd both settle down, he told himself. Their attraction, without anything to nurture it, would surely fade. Perhaps he'd take a business trip to the US, check on some of his properties in development there. Give them both a chance to cool off. An opportunity to forget.

Except Luca didn't think he'd ever forget the feel of Hannah's slender body yielding to his, or, more worryingly, the way she'd held him when he'd been so angry and defeated, the sweet, heartfelt way she'd comforted him. That was something he definitely needed to forget.

Abruptly Luca rose from his desk to stare out at the bustling city streets. He wasn't used to craving another person's company or comfort. He'd lived his life alone, ever since his mother had died, battling his way through boarding school and foster care, and even before then, when she'd been too busy or despairing to care for him.

He'd chosen to lift his chin and ignore the taunts and scorn that had been heaped upon him as a bastard growing up fatherless in a remote Sicilian village. He'd pretended the snubs and jibes of the entitled boys at school had bounced off him. He'd always acted as if he didn't care and he'd almost convinced himself he didn't…until he'd come face to face with Andrew Tyson, the man who had rejected him once already. His father.

Letting out a shuddering breath, Luca turned from the window. In a week or so Tyson would seal the property deal, and he'd be the owner of the resorts his father's legitimate children had refused to take on. He'd have control of the inheritance that would have been his, as firstborn son, if Tyson, the alleged family man, had deigned to marry the woman he'd impregnated.

Then he would finally have his revenge.

In the meantime, he needed to get hold of his rampaging libido and shut Hannah Stewart firmly back in the box where she belonged: as his PA, an employee like any other.

Hannah took an unaccustomed full hour for lunch, walking the streets of the City, trying to talk herself out of this ridiculous reaction to Luca Moretti. She reminded herself of how she used to be with the man, calm and cool and professional. That was how she needed to be again.

She felt more herself when she'd returned to the office, and thankfully Luca was closeted behind a closed door, taking a conference call. Hannah got on with her day and had just about convinced herself that she had this thing under control.

Then Luca opened the door to his office and heat and memory and longing all surged through her body, an unstoppable force.

'I'm going home for the day, to pack,' Luca announced. Hannah kept her gaze glued to her computer screen and willed her hands not to tremble.

'Pack…?'

'I'm going to America for a week, to check on some of my properties there.'

'Would you like me to make travel arrangements?' Hannah asked.

'No, I've taken care of it myself.' He paused, and Hannah forced herself to meet his iron gaze. 'This thing between us, Hannah. It will fade.'

Hannah didn't know whether to be gratified or embarrassed that he was acknowledging it. Was he actually saying that he felt it too, as much as she did? 'Of course,' she managed. 'I'm sorry, I don't mean things to be awkward.'

Luca shrugged. 'It never should have happened. I'm sorry it did.'

Ouch. 'Of course,' Hannah said stiffly, trying to keep the hurt from her voice. She shouldn't care. She really shouldn't.

'But,' he continued, his voice and expression both inflexible, 'you will tell me if there is a result?'

A result? It took Hannah a second to realise he meant a pregnancy. 'I told you I would. But I don't think—'

'Good.' For a second she thought she saw regret in his eyes, longing in his face. But no, she was imagining it; he looked as hard and unyielding as ever as he nodded once in farewell and then walked out of the office.

Hannah spent the week trying to get on with her life. She spring-cleaned her house and bought several new outfits and had her hair and nails done, not for Luca Moretti's sake, but her own. She took Jamie to the cinema and the park on the weekend, and told herself she was blessed in so many ways, and she didn't need anything more in her life. Certainly not a man who would only break her heart—again.

At least, she discovered a few days after Luca had left, she wasn't pregnant. The realisation brought relief that was tinged by a little impractical disappointment. Honestly, what on earth would she have done with another baby? It was hard enough being a single mum to one child.

The day Luca arrived back at work she'd dressed carefully in one of her new outfits, a slim-fitting dress in silvery grey silk with a tailored black blazer. She had her hair in a more glamorous chignon rather than her usual practical ponytail, and she felt polished and confident and strong.

Then Luca walked through the lift doors. Hannah's

heart seemed to stop as her gaze swept over him and she noticed the weariness in his eyes, the lines of strain from nose to mouth. She had a nearly irresistible urge to go to him, offer him comfort as she had once before.

And look where that had ended.

'Hello,' she said stiffly, turning back to her computer. 'Welcome back.'

'Thank you.' Luca paused by her desk, and Hannah breathed in the spicy male scent of him. 'Has anything of note happened while I've been away?'

'No, not particularly.' She'd kept him abreast by email, and even that had felt like too much contact. 'The post is on your desk.'

'Thank you.' Still he didn't move away, and Hannah tore her gaze away from her computer to look up at him. His gaze locked on and burned into hers, and she felt as if she could lose herself in the deep brown of his eyes.

'Luca,' she whispered, her voice breathy and soft. Luca's expression hardened.

'I'll be in my office.'

A week away hadn't changed anything. Luca swivelled in his chair, restless and angry with himself for still responding to Hannah in such a basic and yet overwhelming way. The mere sight of her looking so poised and elegant had made him yearn to sweep her into his arms, pluck the pins from her hair and lose himself in the glories of her mouth.

While in New York he'd tried to distance himself from the memory of her touch by going out with a model he'd once been friendly with, but the elegant, gorgeous woman had left him completely cold. He hadn't been able to summon the interest even to kiss her, and she'd been quite put out as a result.

Maybe, he mused, he was going about this the wrong way. Maybe instead of forgetting Hannah he needed to get her out of his system. He'd been able to tell, simply from that one small exchange, that she still reacted to him just as powerfully as he did to her. Why not have a fling? They'd work out this inconvenient attraction and then resume their professional relationship. He didn't want to lose his PA, and he knew Hannah didn't want to lose her job. Surely they could be sensible about this. Businesslike, even. They'd both agreed that neither of them wanted the risk of a real relationship, so Hannah should surely be amenable to the kind of arrangement he was thinking about. All he had to do was offer.

CHAPTER TWELVE

HANNAH HAD JUST put Jamie to bed and changed into comfy yoga pants and a fleece hoodie when the doorbell rang. She was exhausted, emotionally spent from having been on high alert with Luca in the office, and she wanted to do nothing more than kick back with a glass of wine and maybe some ice cream and watch several hours of soothingly mindless reality TV.

Suspecting her elderly neighbour needed help opening a jar or reaching something on a high shelf—Hannah was called on for these kinds of services several times a week—she opened her front door with a sunny smile pasted onto her face and felt it slide right off when her stunned gaze took in the sight of the powerful form filling her doorway.

'Luca...what are you doing here?'

'I want to talk.' He bent his head so as not to hit the low stone lintel. 'May I come in?'

Hannah had a kneejerk reaction to refuse. She didn't want him in her house, overwhelming her life with his presence, his power. She glanced behind her, as if looking for assistance but none was forthcoming. 'All right.'

She led Luca to the small sitting room, which, after a quick post-tea tidy-up, was free of any evidence of her son. 'Is something wrong?'

'Not exactly.' Luca's perceptive gaze took in the little

room with its worn sofa and coffee table, the small TV in the corner. With framed prints on the walls and bookcases overflowing with paperbacks, it was homey and cosy but a far cry from the luxury Hannah knew he was accustomed to.

'I'm not pregnant,' she blurted. 'If that's why you came. It's certain.'

'Oh.' Luca looked surprised, and then discomfited. 'No, that's not why I'm here.'

'Oh. Okay.' Flummoxed, she gestured to a chair. 'Would you like to sit down?' It felt surreal to have Luca in her little house, taking up all the space and air. She sat on the sofa and he sat in a chair opposite, his hands resting on his muscular thighs.

'This isn't working, Hannah.'

Her stomach lurched unpleasantly. She couldn't pretend not to understand what he was talking about. 'I'll get over it,' she said a bit desperately. 'It *can* work—'

'It's not just you,' he interjected. 'I feel it too.'

Her heart somersaulted at that admission but she still felt wary. She *couldn't* lose her job. 'So what are you suggesting? I need my job—'

Luca grimaced in distaste. 'Do you actually think I'd fire you over this?'

'You might think of a convenient reason to let me go or at least shift me to another position in the company.' The latter wouldn't necessarily be a bad thing, even if she'd miss the status and salary, not to mention the challenge, of being the CEO's executive assistant. And, she admitted painfully, she'd miss Luca.

'That's not the kind of man I am,' he answered stonily, and Hannah thought she detected hurt underneath his hard manner.

'I'm sorry, I'm just paranoid, I suppose.' She spread her hands. 'You hold all the cards, Luca.'

'Then let me play one now. I want you, Hannah. I want you in my bed. Properly, and not just for a few mindless minutes.'

Hannah stared at him in shock, the blood draining from her head, making her dizzy. She could not think to string two words together.

'I don't see any reason why we shouldn't have an affair,' Luca stated. 'We're obviously attracted to one another, and those feelings are not going away. I think it would be far better to explore this mutual attraction to our satisfaction, and then part on good terms.' His eyes glittered as he pinned her with his stare. 'I'm a very considerate and generous lover, Hannah.'

'I know you are,' she answered numbly. The shock was dissipating, replaced by anger, and, far worse, hurt. 'I've arranged the courier from Tiffany & Co. enough times to realise,' she added tartly.

Luca didn't look remotely abashed at this statement. 'Then you agree?'

'To what, exactly? Being your mistress?' Her voice rang out, making him blink in surprise. Hannah held on to her rage. Better to be angry than to break down into tears, bitterly disappointed that *this* was what he was offering her. No-strings sex. How could she even be surprised?

'"Mistress" is an outdated term,' Luca observed. 'And not one I'm entirely comfortable with.'

'But isn't that what you have? Mistresses?'

'Lovers,' he corrected swiftly. 'And one at a time. You're an independent woman, Hannah. I'm not suggesting I take that away from you.'

'But what are you suggesting? Because I've seen you with other women enough to know what you want.'

Ire flashed briefly in his eyes. 'I had no idea you were so knowledgeable of my desires,' he remarked. 'What is it that you think I want?'

'Availability,' Hannah answered. 'You like your women to drop everything when you crook your little finger. Yet at the same time you like them not to fuss when you don't reciprocate.'

'I'm a busy man.'

'And I'm a busy woman,' Hannah snapped.

Luca raised his eyebrows in eloquent disbelief. 'Is that your only reservation? Because I feel quite confident that we can work something out.'

'I bet you do.'

'Why are you so offended?'

'Because I don't want to be your bit on the side,' Hannah cried, rising from the sofa and pacing the confines of the room in her agitation. 'I don't want to be *anyone's* bit on the side.'

'You wouldn't be. To say that is to suggest I'd be entertaining other women at the same time, and I assure you I am always faithful to my current partner.'

'Oh, well, then.' Hannah rolled her eyes. '*That's* a relief.'

Luca pressed his lips together. 'What, exactly, is your objection?'

Hannah stared at him, knowing she was being emotional and unreasonable. This offer was *exactly* the sort of thing she should have expected from Luca. It was what she'd been contemplating herself over that fateful weekend. So why was she acting all outraged now?

With a sigh Hannah ceased her pacing and sat back down on the sofa. 'I'm sorry, Luca, but I find everything about your offer objectionable. It's tempting, of course it is, because you're right. I am attracted to you, very much so, and it's hard to ignore that.'

Luca's eyes glittered starkly in his set expression. 'Then don't.'

'But I don't want an affair,' Hannah explained, even

though at the moment she was questioning her own sanity at turning down the most desirable and compelling man she'd ever known. 'At least, I don't want *just* an affair.'

'Ah.' Comprehension dawned on Luca's features and his lips gave a cynical twist. 'So that really was a "maybe".'

Hannah laughed sadly. 'I suppose it was.' She took a deep breath, needing to explain herself further. 'I know what it's like when a man wants you to simply slot into his life, and that's not what a relationship is about.'

'The boyfriend of six years ago?'

'Yes.'

'But you miss him.'

'Yes, although it isn't as simple as that. But a relationship, for me, is give and take. Wanting to be with a person no matter what comes your way, not only in a set of circumstances arranged to your liking. And frankly, Luca, I don't want to be dropped when you've burned through this thing between us.'

Luca's mouth quirked upwards even as his eyes remained hard. 'Maybe I'd be the one to be dropped.'

'Considering how quickly you've worked through women, I think that's unlikely,' Hannah answered. 'You're only the second man I've ever been with. Perhaps I'm responding more emotionally because of that. But the answer has to be no, Luca.' Her heart twisted in protest but Hannah remained firm. 'I want more from a relationship, if I ever choose to have one. I'm not even sure I would. It *is* risky. We both know that. You clearly don't want to take the risk and I'm not sure I do, either.'

'So you want more than I'm offering, except you're not even sure you'd be willing to risk it?' Luca surmised tersely. 'You can't have it both ways, Hannah.'

'I'm not having it any way,' Hannah answered with wry sorrow. 'But I'm definitely not interested in the kind of arrangement you're suggesting.' She took a deep breath and squared her shoulders. 'It's not for me.' Even though it hurt, more than she'd ever admit, to turn him, and her only offer of happiness and companionship, down.

It wouldn't end well, she knew that. She'd start to care too much and Luca would get bored with her. He'd treat her like any of his other women and that would shatter her confidence and break her heart. It was better this way, to end it before it began, even if it felt as if she were being torn in two.

Luca stared at her for a long moment. 'If you're sure,' he said quietly.

'I'm not sure,' Hannah admitted on a despondent laugh. She couldn't keep the yearning from her voice or the desire from pooling inside her. 'All you'd have to do is touch me, Luca,' she admitted, and she knew she wasn't warning him; she was asking him.

Knew Luca realised it as well as heat flared in his eyes, turning them nearly black, as he eased off his chair, coming to kneel before her. She could see the light glinting on the blue-black strands of his hair and wonderingly she reached out and touched the rough-smooth stubble on his jaw. She shouldn't do this. She really shouldn't do this, and yet she *had* to.

'Hannah, do you *know* what you do to me?' he breathed.

'Tell me,' Hannah answered. She felt transfixed, almost drugged, by the desire that stole through her veins at the mere thought of Luca touching her. Wanting her.

'You drive me crazy,' Luca muttered as his hands slid under her hair, cradling her face and tilting her towards him so their lips were a whisper apart. 'You make me lose my mind. All I've been thinking about for the last week is this.' And then he kissed hers, his lips slanting across hers in blatant, primal possession.

Hannah opened herself up to his kiss, yielding everything under the delicious onslaught of his mouth and hands, her body arching towards his as her hands tangled in his hair.

'How can you say no to this?' Luca demanded as he slid his hands under her hoodie, his bare palms cupping her breasts, the friction of skin on skin making her shudder with longing.

'I'm not saying no, am I?' she muttered thickly as Luca tugged the zipper down her hoodie.

'Don't ever say no,' Luca commanded as he pulled her hoodie off. 'I can't bear it. Don't ever say no to me, Hannah.'

Hannah knew she was powerless to say anything at that moment. Her hands roved greedily over his chest, tugging his shirt out of his trousers, for she longed to feel his skin against hers. With a groan Luca tore at his shirt and Hannah was about to tug her own shirt over her head when some distant, desire-fogged part of her brain registered the creak on the stair.

Her hands stilled and Luca glanced at her, his breathing ragged, a question in his eyes.

No, Hannah thought. *No, please...*

The door creaked open. 'Mummy…?'

CHAPTER THIRTEEN

LUCA FROZE AT the same moment that Hannah frantically pushed her T-shirt down and scrambled up from the sofa. He turned, his whole being numb with shock, as she went to the sleepy little boy standing in the doorway. *Her son.*

'Hello, sweetheart.' Hannah scooped up the boy in her arm, nuzzling her cheek against his hair even as she shot Luca a nervous look. 'You're meant to be asleep.'

'I had a bad dream.'

'Let me tuck you back up in bed, Jamie.'

Jamie. So this was the man in her life. He realised he'd stopped wondering who Jamie was, mainly because he'd been so consumed by his desire for Hannah. Now the realisation slammed into him with the force of a sledgehammer, leaving him winded and reeling.

Jamie's eyes rounded as he looked directly at Luca. 'Who's that, Mummy?'

'The man I work for, Jamie. He…he was just here for a meeting.' She shot Luca another look, almost as if she were angry with him. And shouldn't he be the one to be angry? He was the one who had been duped, deceived…

A *son.* Why had Hannah never told him she had a child?

With Jamie cuddled in her arms, Hannah turned towards Luca. 'You can see yourself out…?'

Luca gazed at her for a tense moment. 'I'll wait here,' he answered coolly.

He was questioning that decision when Hannah disappeared upstairs to settle her son, and he was left alone with the ferment of his own thoughts. Hannah had a child. In light of this new information his suggestion of an affair seemed sordid and distasteful.

A *mother* wasn't going to drop everything to parade about in sexy lingerie in the penthouse suite of the next up-and-coming five-star hotel. He might not have outlined his proposal in such vivid detail, but Hannah knew him well enough to understand what he'd had in mind. Sex, uncomplicated and available, without questions, demands, or prevarications. That was how he'd conducted all his affairs. It was what he'd been aiming for with Hannah.

No wonder she'd rejected him.

With a groan of frustration Luca sank onto the sofa. His mind was spinning with this new information. He had no idea what to do with it, but he knew he was angry that Hannah had kept it from him.

He heard the creak of the stairs and then the door opened. He looked up and saw Hannah looking calm and determined, her face pale.

'Why didn't you tell me?' he demanded in a low voice.

'You have no right to know anything about my personal life.'

He jerked back, stung by this biting assessment. 'Didn't this last weekend give me some right?'

Her chin lifted a fraction and she remained by the door, her arms folded, her look haughty. 'Honestly? No.'

Luca suppressed the angry retort he wanted to make. If he calmed down for a second, he could acknowledge that she had a point. He'd dismissed their encounter out of hand last weekend. The fact that she wasn't falling in with his plans now was a source of frustration and disappointment, but it didn't mean she'd been duplicitous or unreasonable. Betrayal couldn't be involved when there had been no relationship to begin with.

He just *felt* betrayed.

'Tell me about him,' he said.

Hannah's eyebrows rose. 'Why, Luca? There's nothing between us. I think it's better if we try to—'

'Humour me.' He cut her off, his teeth gritted.

She stared at him for a long moment, and then finally, thankfully, she unbent. She dropped her haughty stance and came to sit across from him. 'What do you want to know?'

'How old is he?'

'Five.'

'His father?'

'The man I told you about.'

'Your boyfriend? You weren't married?' He heard the prudish censure in his voice and inwardly winced.

'No, we weren't married,' Hannah answered evenly, 'although I think we would have got married if he hadn't died.'

'How did he die?'

'A motorcycle accident.' She pressed her lips together. 'Why do you want to know all this now?'

'I don't know,' he admitted. 'This blindsided me, Hannah. Everything about you has blindsided me, since we first landed on Santa Nicola.'

'Are you regretting ever introducing me as your fiancée?' Hannah asked with a weary laugh. She looked sad, and that made him feel sad. His earlier determination to make her his mistress—and, yes, he would use that word—felt as if it had happened to a different man. Been intended for a different woman.

In truth, though, he didn't regret anything about the

weekend on Santa Nicola. He didn't regret getting to know Hannah, or experiencing the wonder of her body. He just wanted more.

But not that much more.

'So why didn't you ever mention you had a child?' he asked after a moment. 'It's kind of a big thing. Most employers know such details about their employees.'

'You're not most employers, Luca. You never asked.'

'I assumed you were single.'

'I *am* single.'

'And childless,' he clarified. 'If you'd had a child, I would have expected you to mention it.'

She folded her arms, her stance turning defensive again. 'Well, I didn't. I like to keep my personal life private. And frankly, I suspected you wouldn't be thrilled to know I had such a demand on my time. Executive assistants are expected to drop everything for work.'

'And you did drop everything, on many occasions,' Luca observed. 'Who had Jamie?' It felt strange to say the boy's name.

Hannah's mouth tightened. 'My mother.'

'So she lives nearby?'

'Yes.'

Which was why she'd been here the night he'd dropped her off after their shopping and dinner. He sat back, still absorbing all the implications of what he'd discovered.

'Are you asking all these questions as my employer,' Hannah asked slowly, 'or something else?'

Surprised, Luca jerked his gaze to Hannah's. And realised he didn't know the answer to that question. 'I'm just surprised,' he said gruffly, knowing that was no answer at all.

'Well, now you know the truth. And I can assure you, it won't affect my work. It never has.'

Luca thought of the all-nighters and weekends they'd

worked together, suppressing a stab of angry guilt at the realisation. She should have told him she had a child at home who needed her care. He would have made provisions.

Maybe. Or maybe he would have informed her that she really wasn't suited to the demands of the role.

'I should go,' he said, rising from his chair. Hannah watched him, a look of sadness on her face that he didn't understand. *She* was the one who had rejected him. Not that he'd have made that offer if he'd *known*…

'I'll see you tomorrow,' he said and with a brusque nod of farewell he stalked out of the room.

Hannah spent a sleepless night wondering if she should have done things differently. Maybe if she'd been upfront about Jamie from the beginning, or at least from last weekend, Luca wouldn't have made his offer of an arrangement. Maybe he would have tried for something more.

Or maybe he would have run a million miles in the opposite direction. She'd known all along that Luca wasn't dad material. She'd known full well he wasn't interested in a relationship. Her stupid, stubborn heart had insisted on feeling differently, but it didn't change facts.

Rejecting Luca's proposal of an affair made her realise just how much more she wanted—if she dared. Not just with anyone, but with him. With Luca, a man whose heart was clearly off limits.

At least, Hannah reflected, the knowledge of her son would probably put Luca right off her. And, God willing, her attraction to him would fade when it wasn't reciprocated. That was a relief, even if it didn't feel like one.

Her heart couldn't be that broken, considering how quickly things had progressed between them. A little dented maybe, but she'd survived much worse before, and she would again. It really was better this way.

She was still giving herself this pep talk when she dropped Jamie off at school, mentally kicking herself when she saw that his class was having a bake sale and she was the only mother who hadn't brought in a home-made tray bake.

'Didn't you read the letter we sent home?' the teacher asked, her concerned tone still managing to hold a note of reproach.

'I must have forgotten,' Hannah said. She turned to Jamie, who was watching the parade of parents with their offerings of baked goods with a stoic expression that strangely reminded her of Luca. 'Sorry, sweetheart.'

Her little man squared his shoulders. 'It's okay.'

But it wasn't. She tried not to drop the ball like this, but occasionally it happened. Hannah supposed she could excuse herself considering all the distractions she'd had, but she still felt guilty for not putting Jamie first even in such a small matter.

She rang her mother on the way to work, hating to call in yet another favour but also wanting to please her son, asking if Diane could run something in that morning.

'Oh, Hannah, I'm sorry,' her mother said. 'I'm volunteering at the day centre today. I would otherwise...'

'Of course.' Her mother volunteered several times a week with a centre for elderly people and Hannah knew she enjoyed the work. It wasn't fair of her to call her mother away from her own life. 'Don't worry, it's not a big deal,' she said as brightly as she could. And then spent half an hour on the Tube battling a crushing sense of guilt.

She supposed she could blame Luca for this, for questioning her choices, but Hannah was honest enough to admit, at least to herself, that she'd always struggled with working mother's remorse. It might not have been fair or reasonable, but she felt it all the same.

Luca was shut away in his office when Hannah arrived,

and so she got right down to work, trying to push away all the distracting thoughts and worries that circled her mind.

Luca came to discuss some travel arrangements about an hour later, and she instinctively tensed as he approached her desk. She felt both weary and wired, but at least it kept her from shaming herself with an obvious physical response to his presence.

'What's wrong?' he asked after she'd taken down some dates for a trip he was planning to Asia next month.

'What do you mean?' she asked, startled. 'Nothing's wrong.'

'You look worried.' His whisky-brown gaze swept over her as he cocked his head. 'Is it Jamie?'

Hannah stared at him, dumbfounded. 'You've never asked me that before.'

'I never knew you had a child before.'

'Yes, but…' She shook her head, more confused than ever. 'If you had known, you would have been annoyed that I seemed worried and distracted while at work. Not…'

'Not what?' Luca prompted, his gaze locked on hers.

'Not concerned.'

'Perhaps you don't know me as well as you thought you did.'

'Perhaps I don't.' She had thought she knew what kind of man he was. But that had been a week ago, and everything had changed since then.

'So is it your son?' Luca asked. 'That's worrying you?'

Still surprised by his perception as well as his interest, Hannah relented. 'Yes, but it's only a small thing.'

'What?'

'I forgot his class had a bake sale today. Everyone brought in biscuits and cakes, lovely home-made ones, except for me.' She shook her head, almost wanting to laugh at the bemused look on Luca's face. This was so outside his zones of both familiarity and comfort. 'I told you it was a small thing.'

Luca didn't answer for a moment. Hannah sighed and turned back to the notes she'd been making. Clearly she hadn't advanced the cause of working mothers through this exchange.

'So,' Luca said slowly, 'Jamie is the only child in the class without cakes or biscuits?'

'Yes, but it doesn't really matter—'

'It does matter,' Luca stated definitively. 'Let me make a few calls.'

Hannah stared at him in stunned disbelief as he went back into his office. Not knowing what else to do, she got on with making his travel arrangements. Fifteen minutes later, Luca reappeared.

'Come on,' he said. 'My limo is waiting downstairs.'

'Your limo—where are we going?'

'To your son's school.'

'What—?'

'He can't be the only one without cakes,' Luca stated, and stabbed the button for the lift.

Hannah had no choice but to grab her handbag and coat and follow him into the lift. 'Luca, what are you doing? He can manage—'

'But why should he, when I can do something about it?'

'I could have done something,' Hannah muttered. 'Couriered a cake to the school—' Now she felt even more guilt.

'We'll do better than that,' Luca announced. 'We'll deliver them in person.'

The cakes turned out to be forty-eight of the most glorious creations from a nearby exclusive patisserie. Hannah peeked into the white cake box and her jaw dropped at the berries glistening like jewels in folds of perfectly whipped cream.

'These are amazing,' she told Luca. 'And they must have cost—'

'It was no trouble.'

Hannah closed the cake box. 'I'll pay.'

'You will not,' Luca returned swiftly. 'This is my gift. Do not presume to take it from me, Hannah.'

She shook her head slowly, overwhelmed but also befuddled by his generosity. 'I really don't understand you. Last night you seemed angry…'

'I was surprised,' he corrected. 'And I don't deal well with surprises.'

'And now?'

'Now I want to help.'

'But you don't even like children,' Hannah burst out.

Luca glanced at her, affronted. 'Why would you think that?'

'Maybe because you had to make me masquerade as your fiancée to impress a self-proclaimed family man?' Hannah returned dryly. 'Just a thought.'

'Just because I don't want children myself it doesn't mean I don't like them.'

'But why don't you want them, if you like them? Most people do.'

Luca was silent for a long moment, his gaze hooded, his jaw bunched tight. Hannah held her breath as she waited; she realised she really wanted to know the answer.

'I told you it wasn't worth it,' he finally said.

'But what does that even mean—?'

'Since you partially agreed with me, what do you think it meant?' he shot back, his eyes glittering.

Hannah considered the question for a moment. 'It means that you're scared of getting hurt,' she said quietly. 'Afraid of someone leaving you, or stopping to love you. Of loving someone causing you pain rather than joy.'

She held Luca's gaze, willing him to answer, to admit

the truth. 'Well, then,' he said, breaking their locked gazes as he looked out of the window. 'Then you know why.'

Hannah was silent, struggling with her own emotions as well as Luca's. 'It sounds very lonely,' she said finally.

Luca shrugged, his gaze still averted. 'I'm used to being alone.'

She remembered what he'd said on the beach, how he'd felt alone all the time. 'You don't even want to try?' she asked, her voice squeezed from her throat. She didn't know when the conversation had gone from the abstract to the personal, but she knew she was asking him more—and revealing more herself—than just what he thought about relationships in general. She was asking him what he thought about her.

'I don't know if I can,' Luca said in a voice so low Hannah had to strain to hear it.

'You'll never find out if you don't,' Hannah answered and he turned to look at her, his eyes like burning black holes in his tense face.

'That's a very pat answer, and the reality is more complex when there are people involved,' he said. 'Children involved.'

Hannah's breath hitched. She wasn't the only one who had made this conversation intensely personal. 'Luca...'

'If you want to know why I want to help Jamie, it's because I know how he feels,' Luca continued, and her world, which had tilted on its axis for one glorious moment, righted itself with a thud. 'As a child. My mother wasn't often capable of being there for me. Not,' he cut across any protest she'd been going to make, 'that I'm equating you to her. I'm not. I'm quite sure you're a very good mother to your son.'

'Thank you,' Hannah said uncertainly.

'But it doesn't feel good, being the only kid in your class who doesn't have the right kit for PE, or who can't pay for the school dinner. Not that those things happened to Jamie—'

'They happened to you,' Hannah said softly.

'Yes.' Luca's gaze shuttered. 'After my mother died, I had a scholarship to an exclusive boarding school, but it didn't cover everything. I might as well have had "charity orphan" tattooed on my forehead.' He sighed, rolling his shoulders to excise the tension. 'I can relate to feeling left out.'

And the fact that he was doing something about it, trying to make it better for her son, made Hannah's heart feel as if it could burst. Luca was making it very difficult to stop caring about him. One more little act of kindness and she'd be halfway to falling in love with him. More than halfway; she was almost there.

She gave the driver directions to Jamie's school, and the limo pulled up outside the gates while the children were at playtime. They all ran up to the fence, eyes rounded at the sight of the stretch limo. When she and Luca got out, Hannah could hear the whispers running through the huddle of children.

'Isn't that Jamie's mummy—?'

'What is she doing in that fancy car—?'

'That man is so *big*.'

'He's got cakes!'

The whispers turned into excited jabbers as Luca proffered the huge white cake box. 'These are for Jamie Stewart,' he announced in a voice that managed to be both commanding and friendly. 'I heard he needed some cakes for the school bake sale.'

And as the children clambered excitedly around him, Hannah realised that Luca had needed to do this for his sake as much as Jamie's. The knowledge was enough to bring tears to her eyes. After a childhood that had been far too sad and neglected, and an adolescence that hadn't been much better, Luca was finally able to be the boy who had the cakes. Who could make things better.

Jamie beamed at both of them as Luca handed the box into Reception. 'Thank you, Mummy,' he whispered, and threw his arms around her waist, squeezing tight.

Hannah ruffled his baby-soft hair. 'Thank Mr Moretti,' she answered with a smile. 'He was the one who insisted we bring the cakes.'

Jamie turned the full wattage of his smile onto Luca. 'Thank you, Mr Moretti!'

Luca looked startled, and then moved. He nodded once. 'It was my pleasure,' he said gruffly.

They didn't speak as they got back into the limo. Luca looked lost in thought, and Hannah felt as if she might burst into tears. Finally she managed, 'You're a good man, Luca Moretti.'

He turned his startled gaze on her, his expression ironing out to a familiar and heart-sinking blandness. 'You might not think that in a moment.'

'Why not?' Hannah asked, her heart now nearing her toes.

'Because Andrew Tyson emailed me this morning. He wants to have dinner with us tomorrow night.'

CHAPTER FOURTEEN

HANNAH GAZED AT herself in the mirror, frowning at her pale cheeks and sparkling eyes. She felt both terrified and elated at the thought of the evening ahead, posing once again as Luca's loving fiancée, and it showed in her face. She had no idea what to expect of this evening, of Luca. Her hopes careened wildly, and it was impossible to keep a leash on them.

Her mother's eyebrows rose as Hannah appeared in the sitting room. 'This is a business dinner?' she asked sceptically, because the emerald-green satin dress hugged her slender curves lovingly and was a far cry from her usual pencil skirt and silk blouse ensemble. She'd bought it on her lunch break, spending far more on a single garment than she ever had before, and she couldn't make herself regret it.

'It's more of a social occasion,' Hannah hedged.

Her mother's eyebrows rose higher. 'A date?'

'Maybe,' Hannah admitted, and then added hastily, before her mother got completely carried away, 'But probably not.'

Almost certainly not, she reminded herself sternly. No matter how much her stubborn heart couldn't help hoping since she'd seen a softer side of Luca yesterday, Hannah knew tonight was about donning the pretence once more. If

Luca acted lovingly towards her, it was because he needed to convince Andrew Tyson, not because he actually felt something for her. And if he did feel something for her... was she even willing to try? To risk her heart again, to lose someone she loved again?

Because Luca Moretti was a dangerous proposition.

The burden of pretending felt heavier that night than it had over the weekend in Santa Nicola. How was she supposed to pretend to love a man she was afraid she already had those feelings for? She didn't know what part of herself to hide, and what part to reveal. And she didn't like the thought of deceiving Andrew Tyson again, no matter what kind of history existed between him and Luca. The man was kind, with a genuine desire to see a family man take over his resorts. No matter that Luca had a good plan for the resort, lying was still lying.

Despite these concerns, Hannah's insides lit up with excitement when Luca's limo pulled up in front of her house. Jamie was still awake, his face pressed to the glass as he inspected the limo.

'That is a *cool* car.'

'Yes, well.' Hannah kissed her son's cheek. 'Be good for Nana.'

'I will.' His gaze was glued on the limo, and Luca's powerful form as he exited the vehicle and started towards their front door. Hannah's heart flipped over at the sight of him in a grey business suit with a crimson tie. *Why* did she react this way to him, when she'd seen him in such a suit dozens, hundreds of times? Her body didn't care. Everything had changed.

Luca knocked on the door and Jamie raced to open it.

'Jamie—' Hannah began half-heartedly, because she hated to dampen her son's excitement.

'Did you bring me any cakes?' Jamie demanded of Luca, and Hannah put a restraining hand on her son's shoulder.

'Jamie, don't be rude.'

'But of course I did,' Luca answered with an easy smile, and took a perfectly wrapped mini chocolate cake from behind his back. Jamie crowed in delight. 'Share with your grandmother,' Luca advised while Hannah simply stared, dumbfounded.

'What?' he asked as he caught her stunned look. 'Why are you so surprised?'

'I'm just…' Hannah shrugged helplessly. 'I didn't expect you to be so thoughtful.' Towards her son. He was turning all her preconceived notions on their head, and that was dangerous. Her head was counselling her heart to hold back, stop hoping. Meanwhile her heart was doing cartwheels.

'That's quite a backhanded compliment,' Luca remarked. 'But I'll take it.' His heated gaze scorched her for one breathtaking second. 'You look amazing.'

'Thank you.' Hannah's breath dried in her throat. He looked amazing too, his eyes burning almost gold in his bronzed face, his lithe, muscular body encased in a superbly cut suit, every atom of him radiating both beauty and power.

'Enjoy yourself,' Diane said, a knowing twinkle in her eye, and Hannah decided it was time to get themselves out of there, before her mother said—or she did—something revealing.

'Thank you,' she said belatedly, once they were settled in the car. 'For giving Jamie the cake. You're practically spoiling him.'

'I don't mind.' He sat back against the sumptuous leather seat, and Hannah eased away from him a little bit, because the temptation was to snuggle closer.

'So why does Andrew Tyson want to meet us again?' she asked, determined to keep focused on why they were there together.

'I don't know. He simply said he wanted to have dinner with us, to discuss the plans and get to know us better.'

'Get to know us better?' Hannah repeated as alarm bells started clanging. 'But what if he suspects something? We could get tripped up easily enough.'

'Could we?' Luca asked softly. His eyes glittered in the darkness of the car. 'I think we know each other rather well by now.'

Hannah was glad the darkness hid her blush. 'That may be so, but there are still questions he could ask us, about how you proposed—'

'On top of the Eiffel Tower.'

'Luca.' Hannah's breath came out in a rush. 'You know what I mean.'

'Yes, I know you're tired of the pretence, just as I am. But tonight will be the last, Hannah. I'm hoping Tyson will announce his intentions for the resorts tonight.' He glanced out of the window. 'I need him to,' he said in a low voice.

Hannah gazed at his tense profile for a few seconds before asking quietly, 'What is the source of the bad blood between you and Tyson, Luca? What happened, that he doesn't even know about it?'

'It was a long time ago.'

'That's not an answer.'

'It's all the answer I'm going to give.' Luca hesitated. 'I'm sorry, Hannah. That part of my life is not up for discussion.'

Luca saw Hannah's expression close up and knew she was hurt that he'd put her off. But how could he admit the truth? He'd already revealed enough about his childhood. He didn't want to invite more pity—or condemnation, for his plans for Tyson. That part of his life wasn't up for discussion, and neither was it negotiable.

And while his plans for revenge remained crystalline

clear, his feelings for Hannah were more confused than ever. He'd surprised himself by going to Jamie's school yesterday, and then buying the boy a cake tonight. Even more unsettling was the excitement he'd felt at seeing Hannah; she looked amazing in the emerald-green dress that clung to her like a second skin and brought out the golden glints in her hair and eyes. His palms itched to smooth over her curves, to tug down the zip and watch the bright, satiny material fall away.

Nothing had dampened his desire for her, not the discovery that she had a son, not the flat refusal of his offer. In fact, both things made him want her more, which was contrary and frustrating. He'd enjoyed seeing her cuddle her son, and witnessing her obvious love for her child made a powerful ache reside inside him, for what he'd missed as a child himself, but also for what he hadn't attempted to have as a man. The fact that she'd refused his sex-only offer made him respect her—more than he respected himself. She wanted more from a relationship. She wasn't afraid to try for it.

But he was.

It was fear, pure and simple, that was keeping him from asking Hannah to have a real relationship. The knowledge was shaming. When had fear ever held him back? He'd brokered huge deals, taking massive business risks. He'd started virtually empty-handed, a twenty-two-year-old fresh out of university with nothing to recommend him but a degree. How could he be afraid now? And not just now, but all along?

He'd thought staying solitary was being strong, but since coming to know Hannah, since witnessing her own particular brand of courage, he wondered if it was actually weakness.

And that thought was the most terrifying of all. Because if he did try just as Hannah had asked him to, if he risked himself, heart and soul, what then? What happened if—*when*—Hannah walked away from him?

The limo pulled up in front of the upscale restaurant Tyson had suggested for their meeting. Luca glanced at Hannah, the lights from the streets washing over her pale, strained features. She wasn't looking forward to pretending again, and, God knew, he wasn't either.

'Hannah.' He rested a hand over hers, savouring the warmth of her skin, the comfort of the contact. 'I promise this is the last time. We won't have to pretend again, ever, no matter what.'

She turned to face him, her eyes huge in her face. 'Do you really mean that?'

'Yes.'

'What if Tyson asks for another meeting? What if he wants us to come to the opening of the resorts?'

'He won't,' Luca stated flatly and Hannah shook her head, her expression turning wild.

'But don't you see, Luca? The pretence never ends. He might be expecting an invitation to our wedding—'

'He won't. And in a few weeks or months, we can quietly announce our broken engagement.'

'Oh.' She sat back against the seat as if she'd been winded. 'I see. So I'm thrown over for the next supermodel?'

'I never suggested such a thing,' Luca returned sharply. 'We can make it a mutual decision, or you can be the one to throw me over. I deserve it, after all I've put you through.' And yet the thought made everything inside him clench in denial. They were talking about a fake engagement and yet he still felt rejected. Because he didn't want to end things with Hannah. Not yet. Not until…when?

He knew he was being ridiculous. It was better to be safe than sorry. Better to be alone and strong than broken-hearted and weak. He'd *lived* by that. He'd built his life on that knowledge. He couldn't change now.

Could he?

'We should go in,' Hannah said tiredly as she reached for the door handle. She turned her face from him, and Luca felt the loss.

The excitement Hannah had felt at spending the evening with Luca had fizzled out. She felt tired and sad and strangely empty, and the prospect of pretending for several hours filled her with despair. She didn't want this. She wanted Luca to love her for real. She wanted to be honest about her feelings, not play this wretched game—and for what? A business deal that was practically pocket change to a man like Luca?

He hadn't wanted to tell her about his history with Tyson, and his flat, final tone had made her afraid to push. Luca had made it clear she had no rights in his life, even if she wanted them.

The restaurant was quiet and elegant, with each table afforded maximum privacy. Waiters moved discreetly around the room with its frescoed walls and plush carpeting, and the only sound was the tinkle of expensive crystal and silver, the low murmur of conversation.

The understated ambiance reminded Hannah poignantly of that first dinner she'd had with Luca, when he'd bought her clothes and she'd felt gauche and unsure and yet also excited. Before everything had begun. It hadn't even been two weeks ago, and yet it felt like a lifetime. She felt like a different person, one who had lived and loved and lost.

Hannah told herself she was being melodramatic. Two weeks. You couldn't fall in love with someone in two weeks, especially when you hadn't even been looking for love in the first place.

But you've known him for three years.

'Luca, Hannah.' Andrew Tyson's melodious voice floated out to them as he stood up at the private table he'd reserved for them in a corner of the restaurant. 'So nice to see you again.'

Luca's arm snaked around her waist and he drew her close enough so their hips nudged. Heat stroked along Hannah's veins at the contact. The attraction she felt for Luca was as potent as ever.

Tyson stuck out his hand for Luca to shake and after the tiniest pause Luca shook it. 'Andrew.' His voice was even, businesslike without being friendly.

Tyson kissed Hannah's cheek and then they all sat down while he had the waiter bring them a bottle of the restaurant's best champagne.

'To celebrate your engagement,' he said with a smile. 'Among other things. Have you set a date?'

Hannah snuck a glance at Luca, waiting for his cue, and watched as he smiled easily. 'In the summer. You always hear talk of June weddings.'

June? That was only two months away. Hannah schooled her face into a smile as Tyson turned to her. 'Will that give you enough time to plan, Hannah?'

'Oh, I think so.' Her smile felt as if it were stretching like a rubber band across her face, ready to snap. 'With Luca's contacts, things can happen quite quickly.'

'Oh, I'm sure.' Andrew gazed at them both speculatively, and Hannah tensed, wondering if he suspected. What if Daniela had whispered something into his ear? Then his face relaxed and the waiter popped the cork on the champagne, and then Andrew raised his glass of bubbly in a toast.

'To marriage,' he said. 'And family. And true love, of course.'

'To all three,' Hannah said as gamely as she could, and they clinked glasses.

'Are you planning on having a family?' Andrew asked. 'I know that's a personal question, but—'

'We both want children,' Luca cut in swiftly. 'Two or three, at least. I prefer an even number.'

'Why not four, then?' Hannah suggested a bit tartly. This from the man who had told her less than an hour ago that he didn't want children at all.

Luca slid her a burning glance. 'Four it is, then.'

And just like that she imagined a dark-haired baby in her arms, a toddler on Luca's shoulders, which was idiotic. This was *pretend*.

'Good thing they come one at a time,' Andrew said with a laugh. 'Generally speaking.'

They ordered their food then, and Hannah tried to relax. Tried not to take every smiling glance or casual caress that Luca gave her like a dagger to the heart, but they hurt all the same. Because he was only acting for Andrew Tyson's sake, and yet no amount of reminders could keep her body from responding, her heart from yearning.

When he held her hand throughout the first course, and gave her a bite of his dessert as he smiled into her eyes, and referenced an in-joke she hadn't even known they'd had…all of it made her feel a potent, impossible mixture of hope and despair. This wasn't real, she knew that, and yet it *felt* real. She wanted it to be real.

By the end of the evening her nerves were well and truly frayed. Andrew had remained jovial, Luca loving. Hannah had been the only one who had seemed to feel the strain.

As they were settling the bill she excused herself to go to the ladies'. She needed a break from the play-acting. In the bathroom mirror her face looked pale, her eyes too dark. She touched up her make-up and tried to find a smile. Not much longer now, a thought that brought both relief and disappointment. As soon as they left the restaurant, would Luca revert to his normal, businesslike self?

Luca and Tyson were shaking hands as she came out of the bathroom. 'I'll be in touch soon,' Tyson promised.

'Has he not told you for certain yet?' Hannah asked as they left the restaurant for the waiting limo. Luca opened the door for her before sliding in beside her.

'Not yet, but I think it's almost certain.'

'Why did he want to see us?'

'To make sure he's making the right decision, I suppose.'

The limo pulled away from the kerb and in the wash of streetlights Hannah saw the lines of tension bracketing Luca's mouth and eyes.

'At least it's over,' she said quietly.

He glanced at her, a frown pulling his eyebrows together. 'You didn't enjoy it.'

It was a statement, and one Hannah couldn't contradict, at least not completely. 'I'm tired of pretending,' she said. 'You know that.' But that wasn't the whole truth, and the events of the evening, as well as the past couple of weeks, compelled her to continue. 'But it's not just that. I don't like pretending, Luca. With you.' She took a deep breath and turned away so he couldn't see the tears sparkling on her lashes. 'It hurts.'

Luca was silent for so long Hannah was afraid she'd appalled him with her honesty, and yet she felt too sad to be embarrassed. This hurt past mere humiliation.

'Hannah.' He cupped her cheek in his palm, turning her face so she was looking at him. He caught the tear trembling on her lash with his thumb. 'Don't cry. I can't stand it if you cry.' His other hand came up to cup her face, and his voice came out on a groan. 'I can't stand the thought of hurting you,' he said, and then he kissed her.

CHAPTER FIFTEEN

LUCA'S LIPS CRASHED down on Hannah's and it felt like coming home. Her mouth opened under his and her hands clutched his lapels. He heard her soft moan and it incited him further. He wanted her. He *needed* her.

'Luca...' she muttered and he pulled her to him, his hands sliding over the slippery satin, anchoring on her hips, wanting to keep her as close as possible.

She pressed against him, the softest part of her arching against him so he could barely restrain himself from peeling her dress away from her body and burying himself inside her warmth.

The limo began to slow to a stop and with a gasp Hannah pulled back, her face flushed, her lips swollen.

'I'm home...'

'This is home,' Luca growled, and pulled her towards him. She came willingly, melting into him, her lips finding his as she rubbed against him.

'I can't, Luca,' she mumbled but then let out a breathy sigh as his hand cupped her breast.

'You really can.'

She laughed shakily. 'Is this really a good idea?' She pulled back again, and even in the darkness of the limo he saw the unhappy confusion in her eyes.

Luca took a deep breath, willing the fire in his body to fade. 'It seems like a very good idea to me.'

'I still don't want a fling, Luca.'

He glanced away, feeling cornered and yet knowing it was unfair. Just because Hannah didn't want what he did…

And hell if he actually knew what he wanted.

'Couldn't we just take one day at a time?' he asked. 'And see what happens?'

Hannah stilled and he turned to face her. She looked delectable, half-sprawled on his lap, her hair falling down from its chignon, her eyes bright and luminous, rosy lips parted.

'What exactly are you saying?'

'That I don't want to lose you. But I don't know how much I have to give.'

She let out a trembling laugh. 'That's honest, I suppose.'

'Most people don't start a relationship promising for ever,' Luca said gruffly.

Hannah's gaze sharpened. 'Is that what you're suggesting? A relationship, rather than a fling?'

'Yes.' The word came reluctantly, and Hannah could tell. She laughed again, the sound one of both sorrow and hope.

'Well?' Luca asked. 'What about it?'

'One day at a time?' she said slowly, and Luca nodded, holding his breath, amazed at how much this meant to him. How much he needed her to say yes.

A slow, shy smile bloomed across her lovely face. 'Sounds pretty good to me.'

The next morning, as she headed into work, Hannah was fizzing with both anticipation and anxiety. She couldn't wait to see Luca, but she was afraid he might have changed his mind. Afraid that one day at a time might mean one day, full stop. Last night, in the darkness of the limo, after the intensity of their charade for Tyson and then that passionate, overwhelming kiss, maybe Luca had said things he regretted in the cold light of morning.

Her doubts were swept away when Luca strode into the office and, going right to her desk, pulled her towards him for a thorough kiss.

'Good thing no one else is on this floor,' Hannah exclaimed, her lips buzzing, when he'd finally released her. 'What if someone saw?'

'No one did,' he returned before heading into his office. Hannah sat down at her desk, her lips buzzing, her heart singing with joy.

She told herself to slow down, to take one day at a time just as Luca had said, because neither of them had any idea what tomorrow could bring. But her mind and heart both went leaping ahead anyway. Seemed as soon as she'd got over the anxiety of actually starting a relationship she went tumbling in, head-and-heart-first.

Luca asked her to spend Saturday with him—the day with Jamie and the night the two of them alone. Both prospects filled Hannah with both excitement and nervousness. Introducing her son properly to Luca was a big step—and as for the night…

She just felt excitement about that.

Luca had asked her what kinds of things Jamie liked to do, and she'd told him the usual five-year-old-boy pursuits: the park, the zoo, football. 'And he's mad about planes,' she'd confided. 'We always go outside to look at them heading for Heathrow.'

Luca had typed it all into his smartphone, looking as serious as he did when conducting a million-pound business deal. Hannah's heart had ached with love.

Yes, she was falling in love with this man, and it was happening so hard and fast it scared her. Luca might not be keeping up. In fact, she was quite sure he wasn't. Every interaction that didn't have his hands on her body and his mouth on hers was difficult for him, the words stilted but sincere. He was trying, but it was hard. And maybe one day, even one day soon, it would become too hard.

But in the meantime…

She would do as Luca said and enjoy each day as it came. She knew she couldn't stop herself from falling in love with Luca, even when her mother worried about her, even when she stared at her son's sleeping face and wondered if she was setting everyone up for a catastrophic fall. She knew what it was like to love and lose. She didn't want that to happen again, no matter what she'd told Luca about wanting to try.

Saturday dawned sunny and warm, a perfect spring day that felt like a promise. Luca picked them up not in his usual limo, but in a flashy sports convertible that Hannah had never seen before. Jamie leapt up and down with excitement at the prospect of travelling in such a vehicle; Luca had even gone to the trouble of installing an appropriate car seat.

'It's perfectly safe,' he told Hannah, even though she hadn't said anything. 'I can see the worry in your eyes. But this car has been crash-tested in all sorts of situations.'

'Is it yours?'

'Yes, although I don't drive it as often as I could. I usually prefer to be driven, and use the time to work.'

'You do have an admirable work ethic,' Hannah said with a smile. She buckled Jamie into his seat. 'So where are we going?'

Luca waggled his eyebrows. 'You'll see.'

She smiled, enjoying seeing this lighter side to the man she loved. 'It's a surprise?'

'Yep.'

The surprise turned out to be a visit to a private airfield, with Jamie being allowed to scramble in and out of planes, from private jets to a retired fighter plane, culminating in a helicopter ride over London. Jamie's eyes were huge as he pressed his face to the window and Luca pointed out the London Eye, Big Ben. Hannah's heart felt so full she couldn't keep from grinning. From squeezing Luca's hand the whole ride, simply because she needed to show him how much he meant to her.

They had a luxurious picnic lunch that Luca had arranged on a field overlooking the planes, and as Jamie cavorted around, running off his excess energy, Hannah turned to Luca and put her hand over his.

'Thank you. This day has been amazing. Jamie will remember it for ever.' She squeezed his hand. 'But, you know, the park or the zoo would have been fine, too.'

'I know not every day can be like this,' Luca admitted wryly. 'But I suppose I wanted to make a good first impression.'

'Trust me, you'd already done that with the cakes.' She paused, her hand still over his, longing to know more about this man her heart had already yielded to. 'How is it you grew up with so little and yet now you have so much?'

Luca shrugged. 'Hard work, a lot of determination, and a good dose of luck.'

'Where did you grow up?' Hannah asked. 'I'm ashamed to admit I don't even know.'

'A small village in Sicily.' Luca's expression closed, and Hannah knew this had to be hard for him. 'My mother was unwed when she had me, and in that kind of remote, traditional community we both suffered badly, albeit in different ways.'

'Oh, Luca, I'm sorry.' Now she understood why he'd asked if she'd been married when she'd had Jamie.

'It made me determined to escape.'

'And foster care? Was that hard?'

He shrugged, the negligent movement belying the deep emotion she saw fermenting in his eyes. 'It was what it was. A home for orphan boys in rural Sicily—what do you expect? But I had a good teacher and he encouraged me to apply for a scholarship. From there I went to university, and when I was twenty-two I bought my first property, a falling-down building in one of the worst districts in Naples.'

'And what did you do with it?' she asked, intrigued.

'I developed it into a halfway house for homeless teens and sold it to the government.'

'You've never forgotten your roots,' Hannah said slowly. She'd known that Luca had been committed to certain principles in all of his property deals. She just hadn't understood what had motivated him.

'I never have,' Luca agreed, his voice going a bit flat. 'And I never will.' His tone had turned ruthless, almost menacing, and it made Hannah afraid to ask any more questions. In any case, Luca asked one instead. 'Tell me about Jamie's father.'

Hannah tensed even though she knew he had a right to ask the question. 'What about him?'

'Did you love him?'

'Yes, but it feels a long time ago now.'

'You told me you knew what it felt like for someone to expect you to slot in his life.'

Hannah sighed. 'Yes, that was what Ben expected, and I didn't realise it until I stopped.'

'What do you mean?'

She hesitated, not wanting to access all these old memories yet accepting that Luca had a right to the truth. 'I met Ben while in college. He had dreams of travelling afterwards, seeing the world. When we'd started dating we planned this carefree life, traipsing around Europe and Asia, taking jobs as we could, living totally free.'

Luca studied her, his gaze both serious and intent. 'And then what happened?'

'And then I fell pregnant. Accidentally. And I realised

that I wanted to keep the baby, that Ben's dreams of travelling the world weren't really my dreams, even though I'd convinced myself they were. I'd never been anywhere, as you know, and I liked the idea of an adventure. I just liked the idea of a bigger adventure, of being a mother, better. I couldn't turn away from that.'

'And how did… Ben react?'

'He wasn't pleased, to say the least. He was furious with me, and he demanded I have an abortion.' She tucked her knees up to her chest, resting her chin on top as she recalled that last, awful confrontation, felt the ensuing, needling guilt. 'I could sympathise with him a little, because I'd done a complete about-face, and now wanted something we'd both agreed to *not* wanting, at least not for a long while.' She paused, her gaze unfocused as she recalled Ben's parting words. *I'll damn well go alone, then.*

'Hannah?' Luca's voice was gentle, breaking into her unhappy thoughts. He squeezed her fingers. 'What happened?'

'We had a huge row. He said he was going to travel anyway, and leave me behind. And then he stormed out and jumped onto his motorcycle, and twenty minutes later crashed into a lorry. He died instantly.' She raised her eyes, giving Luca a sorrowful smile. 'I've chosen to believe that he might have come round. He was shocked, and understandably so, and he always did have a temper. And I felt terribly guilty, still do really, for yelling right back at him. But he would have come round. He wouldn't have left me or our child, not if he had a choice.' Luca didn't answer and Hannah let out a wobbly laugh. 'You probably don't believe that. And maybe he wouldn't have, but I don't want Jamie to know that about his father. You're actually the only person I've told.'

'Not even your mother…?'

'I didn't want her to think badly of Jamie's father…and I

felt guilty for my part in the whole mess.' She sighed. 'But it did make me realise what I wanted a relationship to be, and it's not simply wanting to be with someone when they go along with your plans. It's wanting to be with someone *whatever* the plans. Because plans fall apart. People change. I've learned that lesson more than once.'

Luca turned her hand over, stroking her palm with his thumb. 'So have I.'

'I don't want to rush you,' Hannah blurted. 'I know this is new…for both of us. But with Jamie involved…'

'I understand.'

'It can't all be fancy cakes and helicopter rides.'

'I know.' Luca's expression turned distant. 'But I can't help but want to give Jamie some of the things I never had.' He gave her a quick, reassuring smile. 'I won't spoil him, I promise.'

'I know you won't. I can't believe we're even talking about this. You've exceeded my expectations in so many ways,' she admitted with a laugh. 'I should have told you I had a child ages ago.'

'I would have reacted differently,' Luca said sombrely. 'You've changed me, Hannah.'

Her heart lifted and she lifted his hand to her mouth to press a kiss to his palm. 'Not too much, though. Because I like you the way you are.'

'Just enough,' Luca assured her, and then leaned across to kiss her tenderly.

Jamie fell asleep on the way back home, and Luca carried him inside to a waiting Diane.

'Have fun,' Diane said, kissing her daughter on the cheek, and then Hannah was back in the sports car with Luca driving to his flat in Mayfair.

She'd never been to his home before, had no idea what to expect. She'd been touched that Luca had wanted to bring her there, and not to some anonymous luxury hotel. He was inviting her into his life in so many ways.

As excited as she was to be alone with Luca, she was also incredibly nervous. The last and only time they'd made love it had been hurried and desperate, a moment of passion neither of them had been expecting. Tonight would be completely different…a deliberate coming together and giving of themselves. Hannah didn't want to disappoint him.

'I feel a little nervous,' she admitted after Luca had parked the car in the underground garage and they were riding up the lift to his penthouse flat.

'Nervous? Why?'

'Because this is different. What if…what if I'm not good enough?'

Luca's eyebrows rose nearly to his hairline. 'Trust me, Hannah, you're more than good enough. I feel like I've been waiting for this night for most of my life.'

She smiled tremulously, pleased by his words but not quite sure if she could believe them. Luca had had dozens, hundreds of women, and was the most powerful, compelling, and attractive man she'd ever met.

And what was she? A single mum with stretchmarks and a B-cup bra size.

The doors of the lift opened directly onto his flat, a single open space with a soaring ceiling and panoramic views of the city. Hannah stepped out onto the marble parquet floor, her heart making its way up to her mouth.

Luca stepped behind her and rested his hands on her shoulders. 'Hannah. Trust me. I want to be with you more than I've wanted to be with anyone in my life.' Gently he brushed her hair aside to kiss the curve of her shoulder, his lips lingering on her skin so a shudder ran through her body.

'I feel the same way,' she whispered, because how could

she not? Luca was amazing. He'd blown her world clean apart.

'Good,' Luca said gruffly, and slid his arms around her waist, drawing her back to rest against the hard wall of his chest. She could already feel his arousal, felt an answering desire race through her veins, pool between her thighs.

'I brought lingerie,' she told him on a shaky breath. 'But I don't know if I want to wait long enough to put it on, just so you can take it off again.'

'I don't,' Luca answered in a growl. 'Save it for another night.' He spun her around, his hands delving into her hair as his mouth found purchase. Hannah returned the kiss, revelling in it, in him, in the freedom and luxury of the whole evening ahead of them.

Still kissing her, Luca backed her towards his bedroom, separated from the living area by linen-covered screens. The bedroom contained nothing but a massive bed, the navy silk duvet stretched invitingly across. With a little smile Luca pushed her back onto it, and then covered her body with his own.

They kissed and kissed, legs and limbs tangling, hands smoothing over every body part they could find. Laughing, both of them, breathless with anticipation and joy.

After a few frenzied moments Luca rolled away, his breath ragged. 'We don't need to rush.'

'I rather feel like rushing,' Hannah admitted. Every part of her ached with the need for Luca to touch her, and, more than that, to feel that glorious sense of completion and unity she'd felt before.

'Well,' Luca answered as he rolled back to rest lightly on top of her. 'You can't always have everything you want.' He popped the button on her jeans and ran his hand lightly over her belly. 'Sometimes you have to be patient.'

'Are you going to teach me, then?' Hannah asked, her

breath coming out in a shudder as Luca tugged down her zip.

'If I can,' he admitted and pressed a kiss to her belly. 'If I can be patient myself. I want you so very much, Hannah.'

His heartfelt words made her heart sing even as his hands made her body burn. He stripped off her clothes and then it was her turn to unbutton his shirt, tug down his jeans. She ran her hands over the sculpted muscles she'd only glimpsed in the dark.

'You really are the most beautiful man. It's most unfair,' she complained laughingly.

'Unfair? Do you really want to look like me?'

She curled a hand around his impressive biceps as his mouth dipped to her breasts. 'No,' she confessed breathlessly, 'but sometimes I feel like an ugly duckling to your swan.'

Luca lifted his head, his gaze locking on hers. 'Hannah, you're beautiful.'

'To you, maybe, but from a purely objective—'

'To me, yes. Completely to me.' He brushed the hair away from her face and pressed a gentle kiss to her lips before saying, 'I can't be objective when it comes to you. All I see is a woman who makes me burn. Who cares what anyone else thinks?'

'When you put it like that...' Hannah said, her laugh turning to a gasp as Luca's mouth moved lower.

She writhed underneath his sure and knowing touch as he used his mouth and hands on her most sensitive places. Arched her hips, inviting him to a deeper caress and then sighing with both satisfaction and need as he took her up on her blatant offer.

And she touched him, revelling in the hard planes of his chest, the sharp curve of his hip, and the pulsing strength of his arousal.

Luca groaned as she wrapped her hand around him. 'You're going to kill me.'

'But you'll die happy,' Hannah teased.

Then, finally, he was moving inside her, her body stretching to accommodate him, her eyes widening as she felt him in her deepest part. She wrapped her legs around his waist, her hands clutching his shoulders as he began to move and she matched his rhythm.

'Luca…'

She closed her eyes as she surrendered herself to the wave of pleasure they were both riding to the crest, until Luca touched her cheek and whispered raggedly, 'Look at me, Hannah. I want to see you as I make love to you. I want you to see me.'

Hannah opened her eyes to see Luca gazing at her with burning need, and that blazing look was what had her tumbling over the edge of that wave, until they were both lost in pleasure.

Afterwards they lay in a tangle of limbs and covers, their heart rates slowing as their breathing settled. Hannah stretched and then snuggled into Luca, his arm coming around her shoulders. She felt sated and happy, her body nearly boneless.

She smoothed her hand down Luca's chest, enjoying the liberty of touching him. Her hand drifted lower and he caught it in his.

'Give me a few minutes, at least,' he murmured, and she laughed softly. 'Vixen,' he teased, and pressed a kiss to her hair.

'I like taking one day at a time,' Hannah told him lazily. 'And one night at a time.'

'Glad to hear it.'

'It's funny to think that if you hadn't needed a fake fiancée we wouldn't be here like this.' She'd meant to tease but she felt Luca tense next to her. She rolled onto her side, her hair brushing his chest as she looked at him. His expression was bland, and she'd learned how he used that to hide his true, deeper feelings. 'Luca? What is the history between you and Tyson?'

'I told you before, it happened a long time ago.'

'But it matters,' Hannah said quietly. 'It certainly mattered to you during that weekend. And yet he doesn't even know...how can that be?'

'Leave it, Hannah.'

She recoiled at the taut note of warning in his voice. She'd thought they'd moved past that kind of thing. She'd thought they'd been opening up to each other. She'd certainly told Luca more about herself than she had anyone else.

'Why can't you tell me about it?' she asked, and Luca rolled off the bed so he was sitting on the edge, his back to her.

'Because it's not important.'

Hannah knew she shouldn't push. She might be risking everything they'd only just started to build, and yet...what *had* they built, if they couldn't talk about this?

She took a deep breath. 'It is important, but you obviously don't want to tell me.' She waited for something from Luca, but he didn't reply.

CHAPTER SIXTEEN

'ANDREW TYSON FOR you on line one.'

Hannah's deliberately neutral voice made Luca grimace. They'd managed to get beyond that awkward moment on Saturday night, when she'd asked about Tyson and he hadn't given her any answers, but only just.

Part of him had wanted to admit to her what Tyson was to him, but he'd held back out of instinct, not willing to part with that painful information yet. Not wanting to be so exposed. Now he wondered if he should have, because once the deal was signed Hannah would know his plans for the resorts. And what would she think then?

It didn't matter. This had nothing to do with Hannah. What they had together was sacred, and what had happened with Tyson had no part in that.

Realising he was keeping Tyson waiting, Luca picked up the phone.

'Moretti here.'

'Luca.' Tyson's voice oozed genial warmth, making Luca flinch. Tyson had turned away from him once before, utterly and without any remorse. The fact that he was friendly now, not knowing who Luca really was, made his kindness grate.

'Hello, Andrew.' He managed to keep his tone neutral. When he'd decided to go after Tyson's resorts, he hadn't considered the impact of dealing with the man himself. He'd told himself he didn't care, that he felt nothing for the man who'd fathered him, the man he'd seen only once. Even if the scent of lilies still made him retch. Every interaction with the man showed those assertions for the lies they were.

'I have good news for you, Luca,' Andrew said. 'And I'm sure you know what it is.'

'I believe I do.' Luca listened as Andrew outlined the deal he'd been waiting for: a takeover of the Tyson resorts.

'Because,' Andrew finished, 'if I can't have one of my own children running the place, I'd like to have you.' A sentiment that nearly made Luca choke.

They finished the conversation with plans to finalise the paperwork next week, when Tyson was in London. Luca put down the phone and stared vacantly out of the window at the busy streets far below, the sky cloudless and blue above.

Distantly he registered a tap at the door, and then the sound of it opening. 'Luca?' Hannah asked, her expression wary. 'That was Andrew Tyson, wasn't it? Did he give you an answer?'

'Yes.' Luca forced himself to face Hannah and smile. 'He's accepted my bid.'

Hannah's answering smile morphed into an uncertain frown. 'But…aren't you happy?'

Was he happy? He'd been happy this last week with Hannah. As for Tyson… He didn't feel the satisfaction, the triumph and the sense of retribution that he'd thought he'd feel upon owning his father's business. When it came to Tyson, he felt…empty.

'Luca?' Hannah asked softly. She walked towards him, laying a hand on his arm. 'I wish you'd tell me what was wrong.'

This was the time to tell her about Tyson. To tell her the truth. Luca gazed up into Hannah's voice, saw the concern and care shining in her eyes, and his throat closed.

'Nothing's wrong,' he said gruffly, the words squeezed out of his too-tight throat. The smile on his face felt plastic and he reached for her so she couldn't see how fake it was. 'Nothing's wrong at all.'

He didn't think he'd fooled her because she just frowned before kissing him gently on the lips, making Luca feel as if something inside him were breaking.

'I've got a good idea,' he said afterwards, his arms still around her. 'I have a boring black-tie dinner tonight that I was thinking of skipping. Why don't we go to it together instead?'

Hannah pulled away from him so she could study his face. 'You mean…as a couple?'

'Yes, that's exactly what I mean. I've become part of your world, but you haven't yet become part of mine.'

Tremulous hope lit her eyes even as she frowned uncertainly. 'I don't have anything to wear.'

'Hmm, your last evening gown didn't survive the trip, did it?' Luca teased. 'I think it's time for another visit to Diavola.' Hannah didn't light up at this prospect as he'd expected her to. 'What? You don't want to buy a new dress?'

'You'd be buying the dress,' Hannah replied. 'And I don't want to be treated like your mistress.'

Luca suppressed a sigh. 'So am I never allowed to buy you things? It's as much, if not more, of a pleasure for me, Hannah.'

She chewed her lip, clearly torn. 'I don't know,' she admitted. 'But I don't want to be treated like one of your women.'

'You aren't.' Luca's lips twisted in wry self-deprecation. 'I never even spent the entire night with a woman before you, Hannah. Not that I want to admit that, but you're different. I'm different when I'm with you.'

She studied him for a moment, a faint frown creasing her forehead, and Luca could practically read the thoughts going through her mind. *How different are you, really? Why won't you tell me about Tyson?*

She didn't say any of it though, just smiled and kissed him. 'I suppose you can buy me a dress.'

Eight hours later Hannah stood next to Luca, sheathed in an elegant Grecian-style gown of ivory silk. She'd had her hair and make-up done at the boutique, and felt every inch the regal princess as Luca introduced her to various acquaintances.

'Ah, so this is your fiancée,' a paunchy man remarked with a sweeping, appreciative gaze for Hannah. She stiffened, as did Luca. Clearly the rumour of their forthcoming nuptials had got around. Had they really thought it wouldn't?

'When is the date, by the way?' the man asked.

'Soon,' Luca answered in a tone that brooked no more questions. The man moved on.

'You must really be starting to regret the whole fake-fiancée thing,' Hannah murmured.

Luca shot her a swift, searching look. 'I don't regret anything, because it brought us together. But I'll be glad to put it behind us.'

But would it ever be behind them? This was the danger of taking one day at a time, Hannah acknowledged bleakly. You never knew what was lurking just ahead.

She still felt worried that Luca might tire of her or of the whole 'happy families' routine he'd entered into with such surprising enthusiasm. Maybe she—and Jamie—were nothing more than a novelty.

And maybe she needed to choose to believe what Luca said, that he was different, that he did care. Maybe she needed to believe in him. She'd made that choice with Ben after he'd died, when it had been too late. She'd decided to believe the best would have happened, even if they'd never got the chance to see it become a reality.

Now she needed to believe the best *could* happen, that Luca could be the man he wanted to be. That she could help him be that man. They just needed time.

They didn't leave the reception until after midnight, and Hannah's feet ached in the silver stilettos Luca had bought her to go with the dress.

'You were magnificent,' he said as he opened the door to the limo waiting at the kerb.

'I liked being by your side even if it all felt a bit grand for me,' Hannah admitted.

Once inside the limo Luca reached for her hand. 'Stay the night?'

Guilt and temptation warred within her. 'I can't,' she said regretfully. 'I've been away too much as it is.'

Luca didn't answer, just played with her fingers, his head lowered. Hannah resisted the impulse to apologise. Luca knew what he was taking on. Her responsibility for Jamie was part of the package, and she wouldn't say sorry for that.

'I don't want to be apart from you,' Luca said finally.

Hannah's heart lifted at this admission. 'You could stay with me,' she suggested tentatively.

Luca lifted his head. 'What about Jamie?'

'What about him?' She smiled teasingly. 'He has his own bedroom, you know.'

'You don't mind me being there? When he wakes up, I mean?'

'I don't think Jamie's old enough to realise exactly what it means,' Hannah returned. 'But even a five-year-old will get the message that you're an important part of our lives.' She hesitated, feeling as if she had one foot poised over a precipice. 'And you are, Luca.' He didn't respond and she couldn't keep herself from rushing in with caveats. 'I mean, I know it's happened so quickly and we're taking one day at a time…'

'Hannah.' Luca took her face in his hands and kissed her lips. 'You don't need to say things like that. You're an important part of my life.' He paused. 'The most important part.'

Relief rushed through her even as doubts niggled at her mind. If she was the most important part, why wasn't he being more open? Why didn't she feel as if she could totally trust him?

Time, she reminded herself. It would come with time.

'Let's go home,' Luca said, and leaned forward to tell his driver where to go.

Back at her house, Hannah tiptoed upstairs, Luca behind her. Her mother had left with a smile on her face, glad to see Hannah finally finding some happiness.

Her bedroom felt small and shabby compared to Luca's glorious open-plan penthouse, but he assured her he didn't mind as he framed her face with his hands.

'All I want is you. One day you will believe that.'

'Why don't you keep trying to convince me?' Hannah murmured, and Luca did just that.

They'd made love many times since that first unexpected encounter on the beach, and yet Hannah never tired of the feel of Luca's body against hers, inside her. Now, as he slid inside her and filled her up, he looked in her eyes, his body shuddering with the effort of holding back.

'I love you,' he said, his voice ragged with emotion, and Hannah blinked back tears.

'I love you too,' she whispered, wrapping her arms around him, and Luca began to move.

Afterwards they lay together, silent and happy, needing no words.

'You sign the contract for the Tyson resorts next week,'

Hannah said as she ran a hand down his chest, loving the play of his muscles under her palm.

Luca wrapped his hand around her own. 'Yes.'

'Maybe we could go there one day, the three of us,' Hannah said. 'I'd love to see how you implement all your ideas.'

Luca didn't answer and Hannah wondered if she'd presumed too much. Talking about anything to do with the resorts felt fraught. Then he rolled over and drew her tightly into his arms, his head buried in her shoulder as a shudder went through his body. Surprised and unsettled, she returned the embrace. Luca didn't say anything, and Hannah could only wonder what emotion gripped him. She decided not to ask; it was enough he was sharing this with her, and she knew some things went too deep for words.

A week later Luca shook hands with Tyson for the last time as the contracts were signed and witnessed. Tyson's resorts were officially his.

'I look forward to seeing you implement your plans,' Tyson told him as he closed his briefcase. 'I was deeply impressed by your ethos.'

Luca smiled tightly and said nothing. He told himself that he wouldn't feel so flat and empty once he'd put his plans in motion. Once he'd taken from Tyson what the older man had refused him all along, he'd finally sense that satisfaction that had eluded him. The justice that he had deserved for his whole life.

'Stephen mentioned that you looked familiar,' Tyson remarked as he shrugged on his coat. 'But we hadn't met before Santa Nicola, had we?'

Words bubbled in Luca's throat, thick with rage and remembrance. He remembered staring into Tyson's face, those faded brown eyes flat and hard. *You will leave here. Now.*

A push at the small of the back, the overpowering stench

of lilies from the vase in the foyer. Then a door closed in his face.

'No,' he said coolly. 'We haven't.'

After Tyson had left, Luca looked down at the contract with the signatures boldly scrawled. For a moment he imagined what Hannah had suggested last week: the Tyson resorts as he'd proposed them to be, a holiday with her and Jamie. The family life he'd never had, the *happiness* he'd never had. He had a diamond ring in his jacket pocket he was intending to give to Hannah that evening. A whole life about to unfold, a life he now realised he wanted desperately.

Then Luca's jaw hardened and his fist clenched. It couldn't be that simple, that easy for Tyson. He wouldn't let it be. He'd been waiting for this, working for this, his whole life. Justice would be had. How could he hold up his head otherwise? How could he let go of the one thing that had driven his ambition, his whole life?

Grimly focused, Luca reached for his phone. It was time to make a few calls.

Hannah was humming as she stepped onto the Tube. She'd been humming or smiling or practically prancing down the street for over two weeks now, ever since she and Luca had started a real relationship. Ever since it had felt as if her life had finally begun.

Already her mind was jumping ahead to scenarios she wouldn't have dreamt of a month ago. Images of frothy wedding dresses and newborn babies, a house in the country, a whole life unfolding that she knew she wanted desperately—with Luca.

Her mother had cautioned her to slow down, and Hannah had tried, but it was hard when she was so happy, and Luca seemed so happy as well. He was a changed man just as he'd told her, and she needed to believe in that. Trust in his love for her and not let the small things worry her. If Luca still harboured secrets, he would tell her in his own time. She simply needed to be patient.

Her unfocused gaze skimmed across the train car of commuters on smartphones or reading newspapers. Some distant part of her brain clanged in alarm and she tensed, her gaze moving back to a headline she'd only dimly registered in the newspaper across from her. It was the business section, and in big black letters it blared *Tyson Resorts to Close.*

She leaned forward, sure it must be misinformation, and made out the first words of the news story.

In a shock move by real-estate tycoon and property developer Luca Moretti, the newly acquired Tyson Resorts, a chain of six family-orientated vacation spots, are set to close—effective immediately. When contacted, Moretti gave no comment.

Hannah sat back, her mind a welter of confusion. It couldn't be right. The newspaper must have got it wrong, or was attempting to stir up trouble. Luca wasn't going to close the resorts. He was going to turn them into something wonderful. She'd seen the plans herself.

Despite these reassurances a sense of foreboding dogged Hannah as she made her way into the Moretti Enterprises building and up to the penthouse. She'd known Luca was hiding something, something that tormented him. Had seen how affected he'd been on Santa Nicola, having to leave the table after Tyson's toast. She'd tried to find out what was going on but she'd been afraid to press too hard. But maybe she should have. Maybe she should have seen this coming.

The reception area was empty as the lift doors opened onto the penthouse floor, but Hannah could see the lights in Luca's office were on. She dropped her bag and coat on her desk and went straight to his door.

'Come in,' he called at her knock.

Hannah opened the door, her heart starting to thud. Luca sat at his desk, his gaze on his computer screen. He glanced up at Hannah as she came in, a smile transforming his features even as the expression in his eyes remained guarded.

'Good morning.' His voice was low and honeyed and it made both heat and hope unfurl inside her. Here was the man she knew, the man she loved. He would explain everything to her now. He *had* to.

'I read the most ridiculous thing in the newspaper this morning,' she said, and Luca stilled.

'Oh?'

'Yes, in the business section. It said that you were going to close the Tyson resorts, effective immediately.' She waited for his disbelieving laugh. Willed him to rise from his desk and take her in his arms. She needed to believe this wasn't true, that Luca was the man she'd thought he was. He didn't move. 'Luca?' she asked, her voice starting to wobble. 'It's not true, is it? I mean…it can't be true.' Silence stretched and spun out, started to snap. *'Luca.'*

'It is true,' he said finally, his voice flat. 'I'm closing the resorts.'

'Why?' she cried. 'After all your plans…' She snagged at a fragile thread of hope and pulled. 'Is something wrong with them? Did you discover something—the buildings need to be condemned, or—?'

'No.' Luca snipped off that thread with a single word. 'Nothing's wrong with them besides being a bit shabby.' He took a deep breath and laid his hands flat on his desk, his gaze direct and cold and yet somehow also vulnerable. 'The truth is, Hannah, it was always my intention to close them.'

CHAPTER SEVENTEEN

LUCA STARED AT Hannah's shocked and lovely face and wondered at the wisdom in telling her this much truth. But how could he have avoided it? She would have found out about his plans at some point. He'd accepted that he needed to come clean, but he'd been delaying the revelation because he'd known instinctively that Hannah wouldn't like it.

'This decision has nothing to do with us,' he stated.

She shook her head slowly, her face pale, her eyes wide and dark. 'What does it have to do with, then?'

'With Tyson and me. That's it. Old history.'

'So this is revenge,' she said, realisation dawning in her face. Slowly she made her way to the chair in front of his desk and sat down with a thud. 'It was always about revenge.'

'Justice,' Luca corrected. His hands clenched into fists on top of his desk and he forced himself to flatten them out. 'This is about justice, Hannah. It always was.'

'Justice for whom? For what? What did Andrew Tyson ever do to you, Luca, that he doesn't even know about?'

Luca stared at her for a long moment, his jaw clenched so hard it ached. 'He fathered me,' he stated flatly.

Hannah jerked back with surprise. *'Fathered...'* She shook her head slowly. 'I don't understand.'

'My mother was a chambermaid at his resort in Sicily.

He seduced her and then, when she fell pregnant, he promised to marry her. She went back to her home village with her head held high, certain that he'd come for her like he said he would.'

Hannah's face looked pale and waxy with shock. 'And he never did…?'

'No. My mother waited for him for six years. Six *years.* All the while insisting he would come. At first she told me there were letters. Promises. And then nothing.' His throat worked and he swallowed down the lump that had formed there. 'Do you know what it's like to grow up in a place like that as a bastard? My mother was branded a whore, and I was no better. Everyone made our lives a misery, and we couldn't escape. My mother had no money and she was still waiting for Andrew Tyson to ride in like a white knight on his charger.' Bitterness surged through him, bile rising in his throat, and he rose from the desk and paced the room, unable to keep still.

'What happened after six years?' Hannah asked quietly.

Memories jangled and clanged in Luca's mind, an unholy cacophony of unhappiness. 'My mother decided to find him. She discovered when he was going to be back in Sicily, and she went to his house in Palermo. Took me with her.' He closed his eyes against the tidal rush of pain.

'So you saw him? You met him?'

'"Met" may be stretching things,' Luca returned, his voice sharp and hard, cutting. 'We stood in his doorway while he told us to get out. He didn't even let my mother tell him my name. He never looked me in the eye. Just pushed me right out the door and told us never to come back.'

'No…'

Luca's eyes snapped open. 'You think I'm lying?'

'No, of course not,' Hannah whispered. 'It's just so terrible to think a man like him would do that.'

'A man like him? Do you even know who he is? That

kindly-old-man shtick he's got going? It's a *lie.* I know who he is, Hannah. I've always known who he is.'

Hannah was silent for a moment, struggling with her own emotions just as Luca was struggling with his. He felt so angry, so raw and wounded, and he hated it. He wanted to lash out to cover his pain, and he only just kept himself from it.

'So all this time you've been waiting to get back at him? To take his resorts, his life's work, and ruin it all?'

Luca stared at her in disbelief, even as realisation crystallised inside him. She was taking Tyson's side. Of course she was. His whole life he'd been the interloper, the unwanted. Nothing had ever changed that.

'Yes, that's exactly what I've been doing,' he said, his voice hard. 'That's exactly what I've wanted to do since I was five years old. There were lilies in his foyer, when my mother took me there.' He didn't know why he told her that; maybe he wanted her to understand how much that encounter had affected him. 'Even now the smell makes me retch.'

Her face started to crumple. 'Oh, Luca.'

Luca took a step away. 'Don't. Don't pity me. I just want you to understand.' He took a deep, jagged breath. 'This doesn't have to change anything between us, Hannah. I still love you.' He reached into his pocket, his hand closing over the little black velvet box, its presence reassuring him.

But Hannah was shaking her head, her eyes swimming with tears. Luca felt the bottom of his stomach drop out; it felt as if his empty insides had been suddenly filled with ice water. Hannah was looking at him as if she didn't love him, as if she didn't even know him.

'Hannah…'

'Do you know,' she asked quietly, a jagged edge to her voice, 'why Andrew Tyson built so much into these family resorts? Why his son is a doctor and his daughter a pharmaceutical researcher?'

Luca stared at her, his eyes narrowed. 'No, and I don't care.'

'Because his youngest child died of leukaemia when she was only four years old. And they all responded to her death in different ways.' Hannah gazed at him, her face full of pain, a tear splashing onto her cheek. 'Your half-sister, Luca.'

'Don't.'

'I made a choice a long time ago, when my father died,' she continued as she sniffed back her tears. 'I wasn't going to be angry with him for leaving my mother and me virtually destitute. I accepted that he had no idea he was going to have a heart attack at only forty-two, that he would have provided for us if he could have.'

'And you think Tyson is the same?' Luca surmised incredulously. 'You think he would have provided for my mother and me, if he could have? Because what I saw then was a choice, very clearly made, to get us the hell out of his life.'

'And when Ben didn't want our baby,' Hannah continued over him, 'when he screamed at me to get rid of it and walked out of my life, I made a choice to believe he would have come back when he'd cooled down. He would have married me.' Luca shook his head. He could see where she was going with this, and he didn't buy it. Not for Tyson. Not for him.

'Maybe you think I'm naïve,' Hannah stated with quiet dignity. 'Stupidly optimistic. And maybe my father wouldn't have provided for us. Maybe Ben really would have chucked me over for the carefree life he wanted. But I didn't believe otherwise for their sakes, Luca. I believed it for mine.' He stared at her, uncomprehending, a muscle ticcing in his jaw. 'I didn't want to be consumed by bitterness and anger. I wanted to live my life free and forgiving. I wanted to make different choices, *right* choices, and not be bound and ensnared by the past. And I want the same for you.'

'It's different.' He could barely squeeze the words out from his constricted throat.

'It feels different,' Hannah allowed. 'It always does. But think about what you're doing, Luca. Those resorts employ hundreds and maybe even thousands of innocent people. They could revitalise the economy of so many deprived places—you know what it's like from your childhood, don't you, to live near luxury but never be a part of it? You wanted to change that. Those plans for the resort came from your heart, your soul. They showed me the man I fell in love with.'

Luca let out a hard, disbelieving laugh. 'You fell in love with me because of some real-estate plans?'

'Partly. I fell in love with a man who had vision and hope.' She took a deep breath. 'Not a man bent on revenge.'

Luca stared at her, feeling sick. 'So you're giving me an ultimatum.'

'I'm asking you not to do this,' Hannah cried, her hands stretched out to him. 'Not for Tyson's sake or all the employees' sake, but for your own. Don't let the past define you, Luca. Don't let revenge guide you.'

Luca was silent for a long moment, struggling with all the emotions he felt. Anger, that it had come to this, and fear, that he was losing her, and underneath all that a deep-seated certainty that Hannah would have left him at some point anyway. 'So what are you saying, Hannah? That if I go through this you'll leave me?' He took the velvet jewellery box out of his pocket and tossed it on the desk. 'I was planning to give you that tonight. I want to marry you, Hannah.'

Pain flashed across her features. As far as a proposal

went, Luca knew it was terrible, but he felt too cornered to care. Too hurt.

Hannah's expression smoothed out and she picked up the box, snapped it open. She stared at the ring nestled inside, a diamond with sapphires on either side, for a long moment. 'It's beautiful,' she said, and then she closed the box and put it back on the desk. Luca watched, saying nothing, not trusting himself to speak.

'I love you, Luca,' Hannah said. 'But I can't marry you. Not if you're going to be consumed by revenge and hatred and bitterness. I feel for you,' she continued, tears trickling down her face, making him ache to comfort her, even now. 'I grieve for you and the hard childhood you had. Part of me wants to punch Andrew Tyson in the face.' She gave him a wobbly, heartbreaking smile. 'But this level of revenge? This depth of hatred? I can't have that in my life. I can't have that in my son's life. And I don't want it in your life.' She took a deep breath, not bothering to swipe at the tears that trickled down her cheeks unchecked. 'You're a better man than this, Luca. You're a good man. A great one, and I love you so much it hurts. But I can't...' Her voice choked, the last of her composure slipping away. 'I can't,' she managed on a half sob, and turned quickly and ran from the room.

Hannah wiped the tears from her face as she grabbed her bag and coat. She couldn't stay here. She couldn't bear to be so close to Luca and yet feel so agonisingly far away from him.

How could she not have known?

She'd known something was off with the whole deal. She should have asked him more about the history between him and Tyson; she should have tried to make it better. If only she could have done something before they'd reached this awful point, with Luca bent on revenge and her heart breaking.

Even through her agony she knew she'd made the right decision. She couldn't be with someone who was so bent on revenge. It would twist their entire relationship, their whole future, out of shape. And yet right now the shape she was in was broken, shattered into a million desolate pieces.

Hannah stumbled into the lift and then out of the office building, at a loss as to where to go or what to do. Her whole life was in tatters. Her job, her love, all her hopes…

For a second she wondered if she'd been unfair to Luca. God knew she understood how hurting he had to be. And yet he'd been so angry and cold, so determined not to give up on his plan for revenge. How could she cope with that? How could she compete with it?

Tears starting afresh, Hannah walked numbly down the street, going nowhere.

Luca stood completely still for a good five minutes, the silence of the office and the emptiness of his own heart reverberating around him. Then the pain rushed in and he bent over, breathing hard, as if he'd just been punched in the gut. He felt as if he had. He felt as if he'd had a dagger directly to his heart.

Hannah had left him. Hadn't he been waiting for this, secretly? Hadn't he feared that she wouldn't stick around, because nobody ever had? He'd told her relationships weren't worth the risk. He'd told her he wanted to try. And he *had* tried, and he'd failed.

Fury bubbled through him, adding to the pain and grief. Hannah had no right to judge him, no call whatsoever to make demands. She had no idea what he'd been through, what it felt like to be pushed out of Tyson's house, cut out of his life. He wasn't motivated by revenge so much as by justice. Why couldn't Hannah have seen that? Why had she ruined everything, simply because of a business deal?

Frustrated, furious, Luca spun away from his desk, paced his office like the cage it had become. His office phone buzzed and he waited for Hannah to answer it before he remembered that she was gone. He thought about ignoring the call but then decided he shouldn't. He wasn't going to change one iota of his life, damn it, not for anyone or anything.

Grabbing the phone, he bit out a terse greeting.

The building's receptionist answered imperviously. 'Andrew Tyson is in the foyer, requesting to see you.'

'Tyson?' Luca demanded in disbelief. Had his father come to beg for his precious resorts? Now he could send him away, just as Tyson had once done to him. 'Send him…' he began, and then stopped. Why not see Tyson, acknowledge the defeat in the older man's eyes? Maybe this was the reckoning he needed. Maybe now he would finally find the satisfaction he craved. 'Send him up,' he ordered, and slammed the receiver back in its cradle.

When the lift doors opened and Andrew Tyson emerged, Luca recoiled at how much older the man looked, as if he'd aged ten or even twenty years. He walked slowly, almost shuffling, his shoulders stooped, his head bowed in defeat. And Luca felt no satisfaction.

Andrew lifted his head to gaze straight into Luca's eyes. 'I know who you are,' he said, and he sounded sad.

Luca didn't flinch or look away. 'Do you?' he asked, as if it were a matter of little interest.

'Yes.' Andrew drew a deep breath. 'You're my son.'

Something broke inside Luca at that simple admission, and he resisted it, the feeling that the shell he'd constructed about himself was starting to crack. 'No,' he said. 'I've never been that.'

'You're right.' Andrew moved slowly past him to Luca's private office. After a pause Luca followed him. He found Andrew standing by the floor-to-ceiling window, gazing out at the city streets. 'You've done well for yourself. But I already knew that.'

'No thanks to you.' As soon as he spoke the bitter, childish words he regretted them. 'Why are you here?' he asked. 'And how did you know?'

'I think some part of me suspected all along,' Andrew answered as he turned to face him. 'Some ashamed part of my subconscious.'

Luca's gaze narrowed, his lips compressed. 'Ashamed?'

'I've always been ashamed of the way I treated you, Luca,' Andrew said quietly.

Rage spiked so hard and fast Luca struggled to frame a response. 'You say that now? Thirty years later? You've been *ashamed*?' His voice rang out, angry and, worse, agonised. Andrew bowed his head, a supplicant.

'I know it doesn't do much good now.'

'It doesn't do *any* good.'

Andrew lifted his head, and with a cold ripple of shock Luca saw that his father's eyes were damp. 'I know. And I'm sorry, which I also know doesn't do any good.' Andrew drew a ragged breath. 'I'm the worst sort of hypocrite, Luca. You were right to close the resorts.'

Luca's jaw dropped. His father thought he was *right*? Where was the savage satisfaction of vengeance now? 'You can't mean that.'

'No?' Andrew lifted shaggy eyebrows, his mouth twisting in a sad parody of a smile. 'You don't think I regret treating you the way I did?'

'No,' Luca gritted. 'I don't. Considering you never once found me in thirty years, never sought out my mother… She killed herself,' he told him, the words raw with pain. 'Did you know? When I was fourteen.'

Andrew's face slackened, his colour turning grey. 'I didn't know that,' he said hoarsely.

'If you regretted turning us away,' Luca asked, 'why did you never come find us?'

'Because I was afraid to,' Andrew admitted starkly. 'When I told Angelina to wait for me, I meant it. I was going to come to her. But then my father was pressuring me to take over the resorts and marry a suitable woman—'

'And my mother wasn't.'

'No,' Andrew said. 'A Sicilian chambermaid? My father would have disowned me.'

'So you disowned us instead.'

'Yes.' Andrew lifted his chin, meeting Luca's gaze squarely. 'I was a coward, Luca. A dishonourable coward.'

'And it never occurred to you that going on to present yourself as a wonderful family man was just a little bit hypocritical?' Luca demanded.

'Yes, of course it did.' Andrew seemed to visibly diminish. 'It occurred to me all the time.'

'Not enough to do anything about it, though.'

'No.' Andrew was silent for a moment. 'I never even knew your name.'

'You never gave my mother the chance to tell you.' Luca could feel his throat thickening with emotion, a telltale sting at the backs of his eyes. 'It helped me, in the end,' he forced out. 'I knew you wouldn't recognise my name.'

Andrew smiled sadly. 'And you didn't think I'd remember you from back then? When you were…five?'

'No, I didn't. Considering you never even looked directly at me.'

'I was a coward, Luca. I admit it fully and freely. I'm sorry.' He paused. 'I know I don't deserve your forgiveness, but I will ask for it.'

The softly spoken words filled Luca with a fresh rage that possessed an intensity akin to sorrow or grief. Perhaps he felt all three. 'My forgiveness?' he repeated hoarsely. 'How do you even dare?'

'You're right,' Andrew said quietly. 'I don't have the right to dare. I shouldn't presume. But in the thirty years since I rejected you, Luca, I've realised how wrong I was. I've loved and lost…even my own child. Another child,' he clarified quickly. 'In addition to you.'

Luca remembered what Hannah had told him, about the daughter who had died of leukaemia. He could not quite frame the words of condolence that bubbled in his throat. Suddenly he felt confused, mired in sadness, the rage trickling away. He didn't understand himself.

'I'll go,' Andrew said, rising from the chair where he'd sat slumped. 'I only came to ask for your forgiveness, and to say I understand why you did what you did. I don't begrudge you anything, Luca.' And with one last tired smile, Andrew left.

Luca stood there for a moment, his mouth agape, his heart thudding and yet also strangely empty. After so many years planning his revenge, so long craving for a blazing moment of justice and vengeance, he got this? Sorrow and forgiveness and no satisfaction whatsoever?

Luca swore aloud. The sting at the backs of his eyes intensified and he closed them, willing it back. Willing it all back. And then he thought of Hannah.

'Where's Luca?'

Jamie's plaintive question was enough to make Hannah swallow back a sob.

'He's not coming tonight, sweetheart.'

In just a few short weeks Luca had become an important, integral part of her son's life. *And hers.* How was she supposed to go on without him?

All day, since leaving Luca's office in a state of numb grief, Hannah had wondered if she'd made a mistake.

Been too harsh. Why hadn't she tried to understand Luca's perspective more? Why hadn't she practised what she'd preached to him and been more forgiving of *him*? She'd told him she'd chosen not to be bitter, but that morning she'd acted bitterly towards him. She'd turned away from him when he might have needed her understanding most.

But he hadn't acted as if he needed her. He'd been iron-hard, refusing to change or even acknowledge that his decision might have been wrong. And to close all the resorts…

Laura Tyson had somehow managed to find Hannah's home number and had called her in tears, begging her to ask Luca to reconsider.

'Why would he do something like that?' she'd said, more sad than angry. 'I don't understand.'

Hannah did, but she couldn't explain it to Laura. That was Luca's prerogative.

'Mummy…?' Jamie took her face in his hands, his gaze serious. 'Are you sad?'

'No,' Hannah assured him, but her voice wobbled. She put her arms around her son and hugged him tightly. At least she had him. She'd always have him, and she'd always put him first. It was small comfort when her heart felt as if it were in pieces on the floor, but she clung to it all the same.

A little while later she put Jamie to bed and then drifted around the downstairs of her house, unable to do anything but wonder and mourn. After an hour of simply staring into space she broke down and called Luca. She'd do what Laura had asked and beg him to reconsider. She'd apologise for her own harshness, even as she recognised that Luca wasn't the kind of man to back down or unbend. But he'd changed… She'd changed him.

Except, to make the decision he had, had he really changed that much, or even at all?

In any case his mobile switched over to voicemail and Hannah disconnected the call without leaving a message, feeling lonelier and more desolate than ever.

A few minutes later a knock sounded on the door, a determined tap-tap that had her heart turning over. It couldn't be Luca, she told herself. She was thinking it might be simply because he was dominating her thoughts. Because she wanted it to be him so badly.

It was most likely her elderly neighbour, Veronica, asking her to open a pickle jar. Sighing, Hannah rose from the sofa. And opened the door to see Luca standing there, just as she'd been hoping he would.

It took her a few seconds for her mind to catch up to her sight. Her mouth gaped as she struggled to find words. Luca found them first.

'May I come in?'

'Yes—' She stepped aside even though she longed to throw herself into his arms. She reminded herself she didn't actually know why he was here.

Luca walked into the sitting room where they had already spent so many enjoyable evenings. It felt like a lifetime ago that he'd first walked into this room, that he'd asked her to be his mistress.

He turned around slowly. Hannah's heart quelled because he didn't look like a man who had made the right decision, who was buoyed by hope. He looked tired and defeated.

'Andrew Tyson came to see me,' he said.

Hannah pressed one hand against her chest, as if she could will her heart to slow. 'And?'

'And he asked for my forgiveness.' Luca let out a harsh laugh and Hannah recoiled. Maybe he hadn't changed, after all.

'And?' she asked softly.

'And I don't know what to do with that.' Luca shook his

head. 'I don't know what to do or how to feel.' His voice broke as he looked at her in genuine confusion and hurt. 'If I let go of my anger, what am I? If I stop seeking justice, what do I do?'

'Oh, Luca.' In that moment Hannah realised this was her second chance as much as it was Luca's. She could offer him the comfort now that she hadn't that morning. She could give him the encouragement to make the right choice instead of judging him for making the wrong one. 'I'm so sorry.'

'Why?' Luca asked, his handsome face filled with a new and unhappy bewilderment. 'What are you sorry for, Hannah? That I didn't get what I wanted? But you didn't want me to get that.'

'I'm sorry because you're hurting,' Hannah answered. 'And I love you and I don't want you to hurt.'

His face twisted. 'Even now, you love me?'

'Yes.' She spoke with such certainty that Luca took a step towards her, his hands outstretched.

'Do you mean that, Hannah? Even though I tried to destroy a man's life? Even though I put hundreds of people out of a job?'

'Even though,' Hannah said quietly. 'I should have been more understanding this morning, Luca, but I still mean what I said. Revenge is a road to self-destruction—'

'I know.' His mouth twisted wryly. 'I think I self-destructed this afternoon. Having Tyson admit everything… He knew I was his son, and he was sorry. He said I was justified in closing the resorts.' He let out a weary laugh. 'Talk about stealing your thunder.'

'And what's left?' Hannah asked softly. 'Without your thunder?'

'Regret. Sorrow.' He stared at her, his eyes burning. 'And love. Regret and sorrow will fade and heal with time, but the love never will. If you can still love me, Hannah…'

Hannah went to him then, arms outstretched, voice cracking. 'You know I do.'

His arms closed around, his face buried in her hair. 'I love you. So much. You gave me something else to live for. Something good.'

'You gave me that too, Luca.' She let out a shaky laugh, her voice ragged with tears. 'The last twelve hours have been the longest of my life.' Luca didn't answer, just held her more tightly. And Hannah rested there, content to live in that moment. She wasn't going to press Luca for promises he couldn't give. She wasn't going to ask—

'I'm not going to close the resorts,' Luca said quietly. Hannah eased back to look at his face.

'Is that what you want?'

'It is now. What you said…the way Tyson was…I realised you were right. I would only be hurting—even destroying—myself. And us. And that's the last thing I want, Hannah. I love you too much to throw away both our futures.'

'And I love you,' Hannah answered fiercely.

Luca tipped her head up so his lips could meet hers. 'Then that's all I need,' he said softly.

EPILOGUE

Hannah opened the French window of the villa and stepped out onto the silky sand. The waves were shooshing gently onto the beach; the sky was a brilliant blue above. Behind her she could hear Jamie scampering around, exclaiming over everything, and Luca's answering chuckle.

They'd arrived at the newly renovated Tyson resort on Tenerife that morning, and Jamie hadn't stopped for a second. Fortunately Luca had the energy to keep up with his newly adopted son.

This was their honeymoon, taken with Jamie after a wedding in London and a weekend just the two of them in Paris. It had been the wedding she'd always wanted, with family and friends and a gorgeous white dress from Diavola. Jamie had been the ring bearer and Andrew Tyson and his family had been among the guests. It had been another step onto the road to both healing and happiness.

The weekend in Paris had been glorious, too. Luca had surprised her by renting out the Eiffel Tower just as she'd dreamed up on Santa Nicola, and they'd danced alone on the terrace with the stars spangled above them, their hearts full to overflowing…just as they were now.

Hannah let out a sigh, the sound replete with both contentment and thankfulness.

'Now, that was quite a sigh, Signora Moretti.' Luca

stepped out onto the sand, standing behind her as he rested his hands on her shoulders.

Hannah leaned her head against the solid wall of his chest. 'It was a happy sound,' she assured him.

'I'm glad to hear it.' Luca slid his arms around her waist. 'Because I'm happy. Happier than I ever thought I had a right to be.'

The last year had been full of blessings and challenges as Luca had reopened the Tyson resorts and made steps to building a relationship with his father as well as being a father to Jamie. They'd become a family, a proper one, strong and loving, and Hannah had hopes that they would add a fourth person to their little tribe before too long.

She'd continued to work for Moretti Enterprises, and to enjoy the challenges of her job, although she'd reduced her hours to spend more time with Jamie. It hadn't always been easy, learning and loving and changing, but it had been wonderful.

Luca tilted her head up to brush her lips in a kiss. 'To think that just over a year ago we were on a beach like this one, but only pretending. Although perhaps not as much as I thought I was.'

Hannah laughed softly. 'Are you rewriting history?'

'No. I think I was taken with you from the moment I saw you try on that dress. It was as if a switch flipped inside me. I started seeing you differently. I started feeling different myself.'

'I did too,' Hannah admitted. 'I was quite annoyed by it, actually.'

Luca laughed at that. 'As long as you're not annoyed now.'

'Annoyed?' Hannah smiled and shook her head. 'No, I'm overwhelmingly happy and thankful that you love me as much as I love you.'

'More,' Luca assured her, and pulled her to him. 'I love you more.'

'I don't think that's possible,' Hannah murmured, her head tilting back as Luca kissed her.

'Then we'll call it even,' Luca murmured, and deepened the kiss.

* * * * *